The *Val*
of a

Enid Blyton, who died in 1968, is one of the most successful children's authors of all time. She wrote over seven hundred books, which have been translated into more than 40 languages and have sold more than 400 million copies around the world. Enid Blyton's stories of magic, adventure and friendship continue to enchant children the world over. Enid Blyton's beloved works include The Famous Five, Malory Towers, The Faraway Tree and the Adventure series.

Titles in the Adventure series:

The *Valley* of adventure

Enid Blyton

MACMILLAN CHILDREN'S BOOKS

First published 1947 by Macmillan Children's Books
Published 2007 by Macmillan Children's Books

This edition published 2011 by Macmillan Children's Books
a division of Macmillan Publishers Limited
20 New Wharf Road, London N1 9RR
Basingstoke and Oxford
Associated companies throughout the world
www.panmacmillan.com

ISBN 978-1-4472-0525-8

2

A CIP catalogue record for this book is available from
the British Library.

Typeset by Intype Libra Ltd
Printed and bound in the UK by CPI Group (UK) Ltd, Croydon, CR0 4YY

Contents

1

Up in Bill's aeroplane

Kiki the parrot was annoyed. She had been left all alone for a day, and she talked angrily to herself.

'What a pity, what a pity, what a pity, poor, poor Polly! Ding-dong bell, Polly's down the well, good morning, good morning!'

Mrs Mannering put her head in at the door of the room where Kiki was sitting.

'Kiki, don't be so absurd! Talking away to yourself all day like that! The children will soon be back.'

'Ding-dong bell,' said Kiki mournfully, and made a cracking noise with her beak.

'I suppose you miss Jack,' said Mrs Mannering, coming into the room and shutting the door carefully behind her. 'He won't be long now, Kiki. You'll hear him and the others any minute. Now be a good bird and don't make any more noise.'

Kiki opened her beak, swelled up her throat and gave her famous imitation of an express train screeching on entering a tunnel. Mrs Mannering put her hands to her ears.

'Naughty Kiki, naughty! How many times have we told you not to do that?'

'How many times have I told you to shut the door, shut the door, shut the door,' answered back Kiki, and ruffled up her feathers so cheekily that Mrs Mannering gave her a tap on her beak.

'Funny old bird,' she said. 'Ah, listen – that sounds like the children coming back. They've been up in an aeroplane, Kiki! Fancy that! That's why you had to be left alone all day!'

'Jack, Jack, Jack!' screamed Kiki, hearing the voice of her owner. Four children burst into the room, their faces red with excitement.

'Hallo, all of you!' said Mrs Mannering. 'How did you like it? Was it fun being so high up in the air?'

'Oh, *Mother*! It was the greatest fun in the world!'

'Aunt Allie, I shall buy an aeroplane of my own as soon as ever I'm grown up.'

'Mother, you ought to have come. Bill piloted the plane and he was *marvellous*.'

'I wasn't airsick, Aunt Allie, though Bill gave me a paper bag to be sick in.'

Mrs Mannering laughed. All the four spoke at once, and she had hard work to make out what they said. Kiki gave a loving screech and flew to Jack's shoulder.

The four children sank into chairs and prepared to

relate their day's adventure. There were Philip and Dinah, Mrs Mannering's children, dark-eyed, dark-haired just as she was, and both with tufts of hair that insisted on sticking up in front. Both Dinah and Philip were called Tufty at school. Then there were the other two, Jack and Lucy-Ann, brother and sister, who had no mother and father, and lived with 'Aunt Allie', as they called Mrs Mannering. All four were like one family.

Jack and Lucy-Ann Trent were very alike. They both had red hair and green eyes, and were so covered with freckles that it was quite impossible to find a bit of pink skin on their faces, arms or legs. It was not surprising that Jack was so often called Freckles.

Kiki the parrot belonged to him. He had had her for years, an amusing and talkative parrot, with a gift for repeating anything she heard, and for imitating any noise, from a sewing machine to an express train. She adored Jack and was miserable when she was not with him.

Jack had a passion for birds, and Philip had a great liking for animals of all kinds. He was wonderfully good with them, and they obeyed him and loved him in a marvellous manner. He always had some kind of unusual pet about him, which caused quarrels between him and his sister Dinah, who was scared of most animals and of nearly all insects. But now all four were thinking of nothing whatever but their glorious flight in their friend Bill's new aeroplane.

Bill Smugs was their firm friend. He and they had had hair-raising adventures together. In one adventure they had gone down old copper mines to track clever forgers. In another they had happened on a nest of dangerous spies. As Bill Smugs said, those children simply '*fell* into adventures.'

Now Bill had actually been presented with a fine aeroplane, to help him in his work. The children had been wild with excitement when he had written to tell them this at school.

'I bet he'll take us up for a flight,' said Jack. 'I just bet he will.'

'We'll make him,' said Philip. But they didn't need to make him, for he was quite willing to show off his aeroplane to them, and to demonstrate how well he could fly it after only a short training.

'Mother, we went far higher than the clouds,' said Dinah. 'I looked down on them and they didn't look like clouds a bit. They looked like a great big snow field. It gave me quite a funny feeling.'

'I had a parachute strapped to me in case I fell, and Bill showed me the ripcord I had to pull in case of danger,' said Lucy-Ann, the youngest, her eyes shining. 'But there wasn't any danger.'

'We flew right over our old home, Craggy-Tops,' said Philip. 'It was so strange, looking down on top of it. And we flew over here too, Mother, and our house looked like a toy one.'

'Aunt Allie, Bill says it's frightfully exciting flying at night, and seeing the little pinpricks of lights shining up from the dark countryside,' said Jack. 'We begged and begged him to take us on a night flight, but he said he would have to ask *you*. You will say we can go, won't you? Golly! I can't imagine what the boys at school will say when I tell them about going up in a private plane, day and night.'

'Day and night,' repeated Kiki. 'Ding-dong bell.'

'She's got ding-dong bell on the brain,' said Jack. 'There's a small child next door who keeps reciting nursery rhymes, and Kiki listens and picks up bits of them. Yesterday she kept moaning about "three blind mice," today it's "ding-dong bell." Don't know what it will be tomorrow.'

'Humpy dumpy,' said Kiki obligingly.

'Humpty, dumpty,' corrected Jack. 'Not humpy dumpy.'

'Humpy dumpy bumpy,' said Kiki solemnly, and scratched her head with a claw. 'Humpy, dumpy . . .'

'All right, all right,' said Jack. 'Aunt Allie, *can* we go up at night with Bill? He's coming to ask you tomorrow, so do say yes.'

'I suppose I shall have to,' said Mrs Mannering with a laugh. 'You and Bill! So long as you don't go headlong into another awful adventure.'

'Adventures aren't awful,' said Philip. 'They are simply lovely!'

5

'Not to the people who aren't in them,' said Mrs Mannering. 'I feel quite ill sometimes when I think of the adventures you children have had. No more, please.'

'All right. We won't get into any more these summer holidays,' said Lucy-Ann, giving her aunt a hug. 'We won't worry you. I don't want any more adventures anyhow. I've had enough.'

'Well, if we *do* have another, we'll leave you out of it, Lucy-Ann,' said Dinah scornfully.

'No, we won't,' said Philip, giving Dinah a poke in the back. 'We can't do without Lucy-Ann.'

'Now, don't quarrel, you two,' said Mrs Mannering, foreseeing one of their everlasting squabbles boiling up. 'You're tired now, all of you, after such a lot of excitement. Go and do something quiet till supper time.'

'Sing for your supper,' put in Kiki. The children laughed.

'You're an idiot, Kiki,' said Jack affectionately. 'Did you miss us today? Well, I was scared you might fly out of the aeroplane in fright, if we took you. But I expect you'd have been quite a sensible old bird, wouldn't you, and sat on my shoulder all the time?'

Kiki pecked lovingly at Jack's ear, and made a crooning noise. She sat as close to him as she could. The children began to talk about their exciting day.

'Wasn't it lovely going to the aerodrome and getting in on our passes, and walking up to Bill just as if we were grown-ups?' said Philip. 'And golly, wasn't Bill's aeroplane fine?'

'I didn't think it would be so big,' said Lucy-Ann. 'You know, it was funny – I sort of held my breath when we started off, thinking I'd get a funny feeling when we left the ground, like I do in a lift – and I never even knew when the wheels left the runway and we were in the air! I got quite a shock when I looked down and saw we were over the housetops.'

'It seemed awfully easy to fly a plane,' said Jack. 'Easier than driving a car. I wish Bill would let me have a shot.'

'Well, he won't,' said Philip. 'I say, wasn't it odd when we got into the air pocket and the plane suddenly dropped down without warning? My tummy sort of went up into my throat.'

The others laughed. 'Mine did too,' said Lucy-Ann. 'I'm glad I wasn't sick. It was a waste of that nice strong paper bag, but I'm glad I felt all right.'

'We went hundreds of miles, I should think,' said Jack. 'I felt a bit funny when we were over the sea. It looked so enormous and so flat. I shouldn't like to fall out over that! What a splash!'

'I bet Mother will say we can go on a night flight with Bill,' said Dinah. 'I could see in her face that she was going to say yes. If only we could! Bill said we could fly to his old home, land at dawn, and spend the rest of the night with him, sleeping all we liked in his two spare rooms – we needn't get up till twelve if we didn't want to. Fancy flying all night and going to bed at dawn!'

'Then we'd fly back in the afternoon, I suppose,' said Jack. 'Gosh, I'm glad we've got Bill for a friend. I do think he's an exciting sort of person. It's thrilling, too, to know that he's always on some sort of secret job, and never says a word about it – always snooping out some deadly secret. I wonder if he's on any job now?'

'You bet he is!' said Philip. 'That's why he's got this aeroplane. May have to take off at any moment after spies or somebody. Hope I'm with him when he does.'

'Well, you won't be,' said Dinah. 'Bill would never run us into danger.'

'I shouldn't mind if he did,' said Philip. 'Hallo, there's the gong for supper! I'm jolly hungry.'

'That's nothing new,' said Dinah. 'Come on – let's go and see what there is. Smells like bacon and eggs.'

They went to their supper. They were all hungry, and finished up the eggs and bacon and plum cake in no time. Kiki helped herself to the plum cake too, till Mrs Mannering protested.

'Jack! *Will* you stop Kiki picking all the raisins out of that cake? Look at the mess she's making! There won't be any cake left soon. Smack her on her beak.'

'Naughty Kiki!' said Jack, and tapped her on her beak. 'Don't eat it all.'

'How many times have I told . . .' began Kiki, but Jack was too tired to talk to her.

'Don't argue,' he said. 'I'm so sleepy I'll have to go to bed.'

Everyone felt the same – so off they went, and were soon asleep and dreaming of flying aeroplanes over the clouds, somersaulting and looping the loop in a most amazing but perfectly safe manner.

2

Bill gets his way

Bill came along to lunch the next day. He had a ruddy face, twinkling eyes and a rather bald head with plenty of hair at each side. The children rushed to meet him. Mrs Mannering smiled at him.

'You gave the children a wonderful time yesterday,' she said. 'And now I hear that you want to take them on a night flight. I can't think why you want to bother yourself with a pack of children like these.'

'Ah – you never know when they're going to embark on some wonderful adventure,' said Bill Smugs, grinning round at them. 'I don't want to be left out of it, you know. Besides, I feel sorry for you, Mrs Mannering, having to put up with them for eight or nine weeks these summer holidays – I thought it would be a kind deed if I took them off your hands for a while.'

'Well, what do you want them to do?' asked Mrs Mannering. 'Just go for a night flight, spend the night at your old home and come back the next day?'

'That was the first idea I had,' said Bill. 'But now I hear I'm due to have three or four days off – and I thought maybe you could spare the children for longer. We could fly to my old home, and then stay there and mess about a bit. There are heaps of wild birds for Jack to see, and I've no doubt that Philip will find plenty of even wilder animals. The girls will enjoy the change too.'

'Oh! It *does* sound good!' cried Jack, and the others agreed. Mrs Mannering listened and thought for a moment.

'Yes – I don't see why they shouldn't go with you, Bill. I know you'll look after them all right and see that they don't get mixed up in any awful adventure again.'

'I can promise you that,' said Bill. 'There are no adventures to be found anywhere near my old home. It's a most peaceful, quiet place. Nothing doing at all.'

'Well, if you promise not to rush into danger or trouble, you can go,' said Mrs Mannering to the delighted children. 'When do you want them, Bill?'

'Tomorrow, if possible,' said Bill. 'The job I am on seems to be hanging fire at the moment, so I might as well take my few days now.'

'What's the job, Bill? Do, do tell us!' begged Lucy-Ann. Bill laughed.

'I couldn't possibly tell,' he said. 'All my work is secret, you know that. I'll tell you all about the job when it's over and done with, though. You'll find it jolly interesting.'

'We'll have to pack suitcases, won't we?' said Dinah. 'If we're going to stay a few days, I mean. We may want a change of clothes – and macks.'

'Yes, bring jerseys and shorts to mess about in,' said Bill, 'and macks too, because it always seems to rain at my home. And, Mrs Mannering, could you spare a few rugs, as I may not have quite enough blankets for so many visitors?'

'Of course,' said Mrs Mannering. 'I'll look some out for you.'

'I'll bring my lovely camera,' said Jack. 'There'll be room for odds and ends like that in the plane, won't there, Bill?'

'Plenty,' said Bill. 'Bring your field glasses too, because you may want to have a squint at the different birds in the hills around.'

'Oh, it *will* be exciting!' said Jack, his eyes shining at the thought. 'I can't wait till tomorrow. Let's go today!'

'The plane's not ready,' said Bill. 'Got to have something done to her today. Anyway, my leave doesn't start till tomorrow. You get everything packed and ready, and come to the aerodrome tomorrow night. Be there at eleven o'clock sharp. I'll order a car to call for you and take you there.'

'What a time to start on a journey!' said Mrs Mannering. 'I don't know that I *al*together like it.'

'You can't change your mind now, you can't!' cried the children.

'No, I won't,' said Mrs Mannering. 'But somehow I don't feel very easy in my mind about it all. Oh, children, you won't go and do anything dangerous, will you?'

'There's nothing dangerous for them to do,' said Bill. 'I'll look after them all right. Anyone doing anything dangerous will be sent back to you, Mrs Mannering.'

The children laughed. Then Jack's face fell. 'I say – what about Kiki? She won't like me being away for some days. Can I take her with me? What about the plane – will she be all right in it?'

'You'd better put her into a basket or something,' said Bill. 'She might get scared at the noise and fly off. She'll be all right in a basket on your knee. We can't leave her behind.'

'Right,' said Jack, pleased. 'Do you hear that, Kiki old bird? You're to travel in a basket – and mind you behave yourself!'

'Wipe your feet,' said Kiki, 'put the kettle on, kettle on! Poor, poor Polly!'

'Idiot!' said Jack, and scratched her poll. 'All I hope is that you don't try to imitate the noise an aeroplane makes. Your express train screech is bad enough.'

They all had a pleasant lunch and then Bill departed. The children went upstairs to put together their things. Dinah put a whole packet of chocolate into her case, in case there were no shops at Bill's home. Jack stuffed a packet of biscuits into his case. He often woke up at night and liked a biscuit to nibble then.

'Better take plenty of films with you, Jack, if you're thinking of photographing birds,' said Philip. 'I bet there won't be anywhere to buy them where Bill lives. It's somewhere buried right down in the country.'

Mrs Mannering came up to see what they were packing. It was a cold August, with rather a lot of rain, and the children would need a fair amount of warm things. They had put in pullovers and jerseys and macks and sou'westers. She added rubber boots too, thinking that shoes would not be of much use if they walked over wet fields.

'I've found you some rugs,' she said. 'You can each take one. They are old, but very thick and warm, and as good as two blankets. If Bill hasn't enough blankets for you it won't matter at all – the rugs will give you plenty of warmth. Don't forget to bring them back, now!'

Jack got his camera ready. He looked out his rolls of films. He debated whether or not to take one of his bird books with him, and then decided not to, because his suitcase was already very heavy.

'Everything's done now, Aunt Allie,' said Lucy-Ann, sitting on her suitcase to make it shut. 'I wish tomorrow would hurry up and come. Fancy flying in the dark in Bill's plane! I never in my life thought I would do that. I hope it's a long long way to Bill's home.'

'It is,' said Mrs Mannering. 'Now let me see – I'd

better pack you sandwiches and cake to take with you for the journey, because you are sure to be hungry if you stay up all night. I'll do those tomorrow. Have you found a basket for Kiki, Jack? And what about taking some food for her? There's a new packet of sunflower seeds come today. Put it into your suitcase.'

Jack found a good basket for Kiki, with a lid that closed down. He put it on the table. Kiki flew over to it at once in curiosity. She hopped inside and looked out comically.

'Clever bird,' said Jack. 'You know it's your travelling basket, don't you?'

'God save the Queen!' said Kiki, and began to rub her curved beak up and down the edge of the basket.

'Don't do that,' said Jack. 'You'll break it. Stop it, Kiki!'

Kiki climbed out and flew to Jack's shoulder. She rubbed her beak against his hair.

'Ding-dong bell,' she murmured. 'Polly's in the well. Ding-dong bell.'

'Polly's in the basket, you mean,' said Lucy-Ann. 'Kiki, you're going in an aeroplane. Think of that!'

The day went slowly – far too slowly for the children. The next day was even slower. By the time that tea time came the children felt that night would never never come.

But when supper time came they felt more cheerful. The car was coming at a quarter past ten to take them to the aerodrome. Then into the plane they would get with Bill and off they would go into the darkness. Somehow it seemed far more thrilling to fly through the dark night than through the sunshiny day.

Ten o'clock struck. The suitcases and rugs were taken down to the hall. Jack's camera was there too, and a large packet of sandwiches and cakes. Jack wore his field glasses on a strap over his shoulder. Kiki's basket was in the hall also, but Kiki was still free. She was not going into the basket till the last moment.

'Here's the car!' cried Philip, his sharp ears hearing the engine purring up to the door. 'Come along! Goodbye, Mother! Look after yourself well till we come back!'

'Goodbye, Aunt Allie,' said Jack, giving her a hug. 'We'll send you a postcard. Hi, Kiki, come on – it's time you got into your basket.'

Kiki made a bit of a fuss going in. She was excited because of the excitement of the four children. It took quite a time to get her into the basket and shut the lid down. She began to shout at the top of her voice.

'Poor Polly, poor Polly, down the well, down the well, up the hill, in the corner!'

'She's mixing up Ding-dong bell and Jack and Jill and Jack Horner,' said Lucy-Ann with a giggle. 'Be quiet, Kiki! You ought to be glad you're coming with us, even if you have to travel in a shut basket!'

All the goodbyes were said. 'I don't like letting you go, somehow,' said Mrs Mannering. 'It's silly of me – but I don't. I've got an uncomfortable feeling – as if you're going off into another dreadful adventure.'

'We promise not to,' said Philip earnestly. 'Don't you worry, Mother. We'll be all right, and you'll see us turning up, like bad pennies, in a few days' time. Anyway, Bill's on the phone and you can always ring him.'

The taxi revved up its engine. It moved off down the drive, with Mrs Mannering left standing at the door, waving. The children waved back, excited. They were really off.

'Now for the aerodrome!' said Philip, pleased. 'I thought tonight would never come. What's the time? Oh, we're early. Good. Got the passes, Jack?'

'Dinah's got them in her bag,' said Jack. Dinah fished them out. They were passes that would take them into the aerodrome, and up to Bill himself.

It was a good way to the aerodrome. The night was very dark. Clouds covered the sky, and a few drops of rain spattered the windscreen.

'Here's the aerodrome at last!' cried Jack, seeing the lights through the window. 'Look at the flare-path – all lit up. Isn't it fine? Don't the aeroplanes look enormous in the shadows at each side? Here, Dinah – where are the passes? We've got to show them now.'

The passes were shown to the man at the entrance to the aerodrome and the children went in.

'I'll set you down here and you can speak to your

friend,' said the taxi man. 'Then I'll run on to his aero-plane and dump the luggage beside it for you. So long!'

'Now we'll find Bill,' said Philip as the car drove off. 'There he is, look! Hi, Bill, we're here!'

3

A grave mistake

Bill was talking to three or four men very earnestly. He waved to the children, a tall, burly shadow in the night.

'Hallo, kids! I'm busy for a few minutes. You cut along to the aeroplane and wait for me. Stow your cases in at the back where mine is. I'll be about ten minutes or so.'

'Right, Bill,' said Jack, and the four of them moved off to where the taxi man had put their cases, beside an aeroplane not very far away.

It was dark where the aeroplane stood, but the children could see enough to pick up their cases. They climbed up the ladder and into the cabin.

The inside of the plane was in darkness. The children had no idea how to put the lights on. They felt their way to the back of the plane and put down their things. They threw their rugs there too. Jack put Kiki's basket down carefully. Kiki had been most indignant all the way.

'Humpy dumpy bumpy,' she said. 'Pop goes the weasel!'

There was a large crate in the middle of the plane. The children wondered what was in it. Was it empty or full? It must be something Bill was taking back with him.

'It's blocking up all the inside,' said Jack. 'We can't sit down properly with that thing there. Let's squat down on our rugs at the back. We'll be quite comfortable there. Perhaps Bill will shift the crate a bit when he comes, and tell us where he wants us to sit.'

So they sat down patiently on their rugs and waited. The noise of the plane's engines went on and on, and it was impossible to hear anything else, though once Jack thought he could hear somebody shouting.

He went to the door and looked out. But all was darkness and Bill was nowhere to be seen. What a time he was!

He went back to his place, yawning. Lucy-Ann was half asleep. 'I wish Bill would come,' said Philip. 'I shall go to sleep if he doesn't.'

Then a lot of things happened very quickly indeed. Over and above the sound of the engine came the sound of shots – gunshots. That made the children sit up in a hurry.

Then another shot sounded – and then there came the noise of someone clambering hurriedly up the steps into the plane, and a man flung himself down in the control seat. Another followed, panting, hardly to be seen in the darkness. The children sat as if they were frozen. What in the world was happening? Was one of the men Bill? Who was the other – and what was the hurry? The first man took the controls of the plane, and to the children's amazement it began to taxi forwards. They were off! But why hadn't Bill spoken to them? Why hadn't he at least looked round to see that they were safely inside?

'Keep quiet,' said Jack to the others. 'If Bill doesn't want to speak to us, there's a reason. Maybe he doesn't want the other fellow to know we're here. Keep quiet.'

The plane rose into the air, its propellers making a great whirring noise. It headed swiftly into the wind.

The men shouted to one another, but the children could not make out what they were saying because the noise of the engine was so loud. They sat quiet and still, hidden from view by the big crate standing in the middle of the plane.

Bill said nothing to them at all. He didn't call out to know if they were there. He didn't send his companion along to see if they were all right. He simply took no notice of them at all. It was very queer and Lucy-Ann didn't like it a bit.

One of the men fiddled about and found a switch. He pulled it down and a light shone out just by the men, but the rest of the plane was still in darkness. Philip peeped round the crate, meaning to catch Bill's eye if he could.

Almost at once he came back to the others, and sat down very quietly. He said nothing.

'What's up?' asked Jack, sensing that Philip was worried.

'You go and look round that crate,' said Philip. 'Have a good look at the two men.'

Jack went and peered round. He came back feeling puzzled and scared. 'Neither of those men is Bill,' he said. 'Golly – it's funny!'

'What do you mean?' said Lucy-Ann in alarm. 'One must be Bill. Why, this is Bill's aeroplane!'

'Yes, but *is* it?' said Dinah suddenly. 'Look where the light catches those seats, Lucy-Ann – they are red – and the ones in Bill's plane were green. I remember them quite well.'

'So they were,' said Jack, remembering too. 'Golly! We're in the wrong plane!'

There was a long silence. Nobody knew what to think about it. They were in the wrong plane – not Bill's at all! Two strange men sat at the controls – men who would probably be extremely angry when they found their unexpected passengers. Neither Jack nor Philip liked the look of the men in the least. They had really only seen the backs of their heads, and the side face of the man when he had turned to shout to his companion – but neither of the boys had felt drawn to the two men.

'They've got such thick necks,' thought Jack. 'Oh, gosh this is awful! And there were those shots too – were they anything to do with these men? They clambered into the plane in a frightful hurry and set off at once. I do believe we've stumbled into an adventure again.'

Philip spoke cautiously to the others. It was no good whispering, because whispers couldn't possibly be heard. So Philip had to speak loudly, and trust that he would not be heard by the men in front.

'What are we going to do? We *have* got into the wrong plane! That's the fault of that stupid taxi-man, putting down our things by the wrong aeroplane. It was so dark that we ourselves couldn't possibly tell which plane was which.'

Lucy-Ann sat close to Jack, frightened. It wasn't very nice to be high up in the air, lost in the darkness, in the wrong aeroplane with men that none of them had seen before.

'What *can* we do?' wondered Jack. 'We really are in a mess. Honestly, those two men won't half be mad when they see us!'

'They might tip us out,' said Lucy-Ann in alarm. 'And we haven't got parachutes on. Jack, don't let them know we're here.'

'They'll have to know sooner or later,' said Dinah. 'What idiots we are – getting into the wrong plane! I never thought of that.'

There was a silence again, with everyone thinking very hard.

'Shall we just stay here at the back of the plane on our

rugs, and hope we shan't be noticed?' said Philip. 'Then, when we arrive somewhere maybe we can slip out of the plane and look for help.'

'Yes – that's the best idea,' said Jack. 'We are well hidden here, unless the men come round to the back for something. Maybe they will arrive at their destination, get out without seeing us, and then we can slip out ourselves and ask for help to get back home.'

'I did want to stay with Bill,' said Lucy-Ann, almost in tears. 'Whatever will he be thinking?'

'Goodness knows!' said Jack gloomily. 'He'll be hunting all over the aerodrome for us. You know, I believe that must have been Bill I heard shouting, when I went to the door to see. He must have gone to his own plane, found we weren't there and yelled for us. Dash! If only I'd guessed that!'

'Well, it's too late now,' said Philip. 'I hope Mother won't be worried. Oh dear – she'll think we've fallen headlong into another adventure. And we promised not to.'

The aeroplane roared on through the dark night. The children had no idea whether they were flying north, south, east or west. Then Jack remembered his pocket compass and took it out.

'We're flying east,' he said. 'I wonder where we're going to. I don't somehow feel as if I'm in a plane at all, as I can't look out and see the ground far below.'

The others felt the same. Lucy-Ann lay down on the

rugs and yawned. 'I'm going to sleep,' she said. 'I shall only feel frightened and worried if I keep awake.'

'It's a good idea of yours,' said Philip, and he stretched himself out on the rugs too. 'We shall be sure to wake up if we arrive anywhere.'

'Anyone want a sandwich or bit of cake?' asked Dinah, remembering the picnic packet. But nobody did. The shock of finding themselves in the wrong aeroplane had taken away their appetites completely.

Soon all of them but Jack were asleep. He lay awake, thinking hard. Had Bill been mixed up in the shooting they had heard? Were these two men anything to do with the job Bill had been working on – the 'secret' job? It might be just possible that Jack and the others might find out something that would help Bill. It was important not to let the two men know that they had some hidden passengers in their plane.

Kiki gave an exasperated screech in her basket. Jack jumped. He had forgotten Kiki. He tapped the basket and spoke in as low a voice as he could, hoping that Kiki would hear him.

'Shut up, Kiki! Don't make a noise, whatever you do. It's very important to be quiet. You hear me, Kiki? You must be quiet, be quiet, be quiet.'

'Be quiet,' repeated Kiki, from inside the basket. 'Shhhhhhhhh!'

Jack couldn't help smiling. 'Yes,' he said, putting his face close to the basket. 'Shhhhhhhh!'

Kiki was quiet after that. She was a mischievous, noisy bird, but she would always be quiet if Jack wanted her to be. So she sat inside her basket, trying to tuck her head under her wing and go to sleep. But the loud sound of the plane's engine upset her. She had never heard such a noise before. She longed to imitate it, but fortunately she didn't try just then.

After a bit the two men changed places and the second one took over the controls. The first one yawned and stretched. He got up and Jack's heart almost stopped beating in fright. Was he going to come to the back of the plane? He wondered whether or not to wake the others.

But the man did not come to the back. He stood up for a few minutes as if to stretch his legs, then lighted a pipe. Blue smoke drifted to the back of the cabin. Jack was most relieved to see the man sit down again.

The boy soon grew sleepy too. He lay down close to the others, quite glad of his coat, for it was very cold. Soon he was asleep. Only Kiki kept awake, cracking her beak now and again, puzzled and wondering what this strange night adventure meant.

The plane flew on in darkness, passing over towns and villages, fields, rivers and woods. It passed over the sea to where the lights of ships shone dimly. Lights of the towns twinkled up, and here and there the flare path of an aerodrome shone up to the sky. But the plane did not fly down. It swept over them all, heading east, to the dawn.

Then, just before dawn, it began to circle round more slowly. It dropped as it circled, and once banked so steeply that the children almost rolled over. It awoke them and they sat up, wondering where they were. They remembered at once and looked at one another with wide eyes.

'We're going to land. Where shall we find we are? Look out for a quick escape as soon as we get the chance,' they whispered to one another. 'Down we go – we're landing!'

4

Wherever can we be?

The aeroplane landed with a slight bump that shook the children and made them gasp. Then it ran along a little way on its huge wheels, and stopped. They had arrived.

But where? Dawn had come, and light came in at the windows, but it was not full morning yet. One of the men switched off the throbbing engines. At once a great quiet and peace came into the cabin. How marvellous not to have that enormous noise flooding into their ears any more! The children were glad.

They heard the men's voices. 'We've made good time – and a good landing too. You brought her in well, Juan.'

'We've not got much time to spare,' said Juan. 'Come on – let's get out and stretch our legs. We'll go to the hut and have a meal.'

To the children's enormous delight the men clambered out of the plane and disappeared. They hadn't even gone round to the back of the crate and seen the children! Maybe they could escape and get help at once.

Anyway they would be able to send word to Bill and Mrs Mannering telling them not to worry.

'Come on,' said Jack, getting up cautiously. 'Let's squint out of the window and see where we are. On an aerodrome, I hope. We'll probably see a mechanic or two, and ask them to direct us to someone in authority.'

They all crowded to the nearest window. But what a shock when they looked out!

They were not on an aerodrome at all. They were on a broad flat piece of grassland in a valley – and that valley seemed to be surrounded on all sides by towering mountains.

'Gosh!' said Jack. 'Where are we? Back of beyond, I should think.'

'We're in a valley,' said Philip. 'With mountains all round – awfully beautiful – but awfully lonely! How can we get help here? There won't be a plane to take us back, that's certain.'

There wasn't a house or any kind of building to be seen. The view from the other side of the plane was exactly the same – mountains on every side. They seemed to be at the bottom of them, in a green valley. It was very strange. Why should the men come there?

'What are we going to do?' asked Dinah. 'Do we get out – or stay in – or what?'

'Well – I don't know what you think, Philip,' said Jack, 'but I don't like any of this. I don't like those men, I don't like the way they flew off in the middle of the night after what sounded like a lot of shooting – and I don't like this lonely valley either. But all the same I think it would be a good idea if we got out and snooped round a bit. There must be people somewhere about – shepherds, perhaps – somebody like that.'

'What country are we in?' asked Lucy-Ann. 'Shall we be able to speak their language?'

'I don't suppose so for a minute,' said Philip. 'But we'll just have to try and make ourselves understood.'

'I wonder what those men have come here for,' said Dinah thoughtfully. 'It seems a funny lonely place to come to. I don't think they are up to any good. I think it would be just as well to get out now, whilst we can, and hide, and then see if we can't find someone to help us. We can report everything to Bill when we get back.'

'That's the best idea,' said Jack at once. 'I'll be glad to be in the open air again. This plane's jolly stuffy.'

They looked cautiously out of every window to see if they could spot the two men. But there was no sign of them at all.

'Better get going,' said Jack. 'What about our suitcases – and rugs – and Kiki?'

'Don't leave them here,' said Philip. 'We don't want the men to guess we've been passengers in their plane. Take them with us.'

So the four of them left the plane and handed down their cases and rugs to one another. Kiki uttered a few words of annoyance at being lifted about like luggage, but only in a very low voice.

Soon all the children were standing outside the plane, wondering which way to go. Jack suddenly nudged Philip and made him jump.

'Look! Look over there!'

They all looked and saw a thin spire of blue smoke rising into the air.

'The men have made a fire down there, I should think,' said Jack in a low voice. 'Better not go in that direction. We'll take this path here – if it *is* a path.'

The little procession wound round some big rocks, and came to where a stream burbled down the hillside. It gushed out not far off as a spring, and became a little stream almost at once.

'We could drink from that,' said Philip. 'I'm thirsty. But I'm not hungry yet. Funny!'

'Well, we're all a bit tired and worried and puzzled,' said Jack. 'Let's get some water into our hands and lap it up. I'm thirsty too.'

The water was cold and crystal clear. It was delicious. All the children felt better for a drink. Dinah dipped her hanky into the stream and wiped her face. She felt much fresher then, and Lucy-Ann did the same.

'The thing is to find a good hiding place for ourselves and these cases,' said Jack. 'I'm afraid if those two men start wandering about they may come across us. Where *can* we go?'

'Let's go straight on,' said Dinah. 'Up the hill here. If we keep up a little we shall be able to see the plane down in the valley and keep our sense of direction a bit. Keep among those trees.'

'That's a good idea,' said Philip, and they made their way slowly towards the trees. They felt safer among them. The men could not spot them there. On the other hand, they found that they could no longer see the plane.

'We can always spot it by climbing up a tree,' said Jack. 'I say – look there – is that a house?'

Set in a clearing was what looked like a house. But when the children got near they found that it was almost burnt out – just a blackened ruin, empty and deserted.

'What a pity,' said Philip. 'We could easily have asked help from the people who lived there. I wonder how the house got burnt.'

They went on a little higher, through a copse of silver birch trees. They saw another building a little higher up – but to their astonishment and dismay that too was a blackened, scorched ruin. There was no sign of life anywhere about it.

'Two burnt houses – and nobody to be found anywhere,' said Jack. 'Very curious. What's been happening in this valley?'

Higher up still they could see yet another house – would that be burnt out too? They laboured up to it, and gazed on it in despair.

'Quite burnt out,' said Dinah. 'What an awful thing! What's happened to the people who lived here? There must have been war here, or something. I do wonder where we are.'

'Look – that cowshed, or whatever it is, isn't very much burnt out,' said Jack. 'Let's go over and see if the roof is still on. If it is, we could put our things there.'

They made their way to the broken-down cowshed. It seemed as if the flames had got hold of one half of it but had left the other half. The roof was almost off, but at the back was a sheltered place, with stalls where cows had once been put.

'This is all right,' said Jack, making his way into the last stall of all. 'The roof here will keep out the rain if it comes – and there are some jolly big clouds about. We can put our things here.'

'The floor's dirty,' said Lucy-Ann, turning up her nose in disgust.

'Well, we may perhaps be able to find a broom or something to get it clean – and we'll spread it with grass or bracken for a carpet,' said Dinah. 'Then, if we spread out our rugs on it, we could even sleep here. We may not be able to find anyone to help us today. We could spend the night here.'

They put their cases in the corner and draped the rugs over them. Kiki was put down on top in her basket. She gave a squawk of protest.

'Do you think it would be safe to let her out?' said

Jack. 'She'll sit on my shoulder for hours now, I'm sure, if I tell her to. She must be so uncomfortable cooped up in that box.'

'Yes – let her out,' said Philip. 'If she does fly off for a bit and the men see her they won't know what she is or who she belongs to. She'll give them a fright if she begins to talk.'

Kiki was set free. She was overjoyed. She clambered out of the basket and flew to Jack's shoulder. She nibbled his ear fondly.

'Where's your handkerchief?' she said. 'How many times have I told you to . . .'

'All right, Kiki, all right,' said Jack. 'Not so loud, there's a good old thing.'

'Shhhhhhhhhh!' said Kiki at the top of her voice. Then she said no more, but just sat and cracked her beak.

'Well – what are our plans?' said Philip, sitting on his suitcase. 'Shall we go exploring a bit further and see if we can find anyone to help us? Or shall we keep an eye on those men and see if we can find out why they've come here? Or shall we just stay here and hide?'

'I think we'd better go exploring,' said Jack. 'The most important thing really is to find help. We simply must get back home at once if we can. Aunt Allie and Bill will be worried to death about us.'

'This is such a lovely valley,' said Dinah, looking out of the tumbledown cowshed. 'I can't think why it isn't packed with houses and cattle and sheep. But I can't see a soul. I can't even see any smoke anywhere – except for that bit over there, where the men are. It's very mysterious. Why are all those houses burnt, and why isn't there anyone here?'

'Well, we've only seen just a bit of the valley and hillside,' said Philip. 'We may go round a corner and come on a whole village. Aren't those mountains enormous?'

'Yes. They make a ring all round this valley,' said Lucy-Ann. 'I wonder where the way out it. Mountains always have passes through them, don't they?'

'Yes,' said Jack. 'But I shouldn't care to go looking for one if I didn't know the way. See that mountain over there? It's got a white tip. I bet that's snow. It shows how high it must be.'

It certainly was a beautiful valley, and the mountains that guarded it were magnificent. But it had a deserted lonely air about it, and even the few birds that flew by every now and again seemed silent and cautious.

'There's something mysterious here,' said Jack. 'You know – I believe – yes, I really do believe – we're in for another adventure.'

'Rubbish!' said Philip. 'We shall find a farm near by, get help, have a message sent somewhere, find a car road, go to the nearest town by car, and from there to an aerodrome. And I bet you we'll be home by tomorrow.'

'I bet we won't,' said Jack. Lucy-Ann looked alarmed.

'But what about meals?' she said. 'We've only got

Aunt Allie's picnic packet – and few biscuits and some chocolate. We'll starve if we don't get home quickly. There's nothing to eat here.'

Nobody had thought of that. It was a nuisance. An adventure was one thing – but an adventure without anything to eat was quite another thing. That wouldn't do at all.

'I don't think we'll make this an adventure after all,' said Jack. But an adventure it was – and they were only at the beginning of it too.

5

A little exploring

The four children went to the broken-down door and gazed out at the towering mountains around them. They seemed to hem the valley in and make it a green prison. None of the children had seen such high mountains before. Clouds hung about halfway up two or three of them, and their tops showed now and again as the clouds shifted and parted.

'It's a very lonely kind of place,' said Jack. 'I bet there's all kinds of strange birds here – but I've only seen one or two so far. It's funny that those men should have known where to land in this valley – that smooth strip of grass makes a splendid landing ground. It looks as if they've been here before. But why should they come *here*? There doesn't seem anything to come for at all – no hotel, not even a cottage that isn't burnt, as far as we can see.'

'Oh, there may be,' said Philip. 'Hey, look at that little lizard! I've never seen one like that before. What a pretty little fellow!'

The lizard ran close by Philip's feet. The boy bent down quietly and his left hand caught the tiny creature by the neck. If he had caught it by the tail it would probably have snapped off, and the lizard would have run away without it.

'Oh, put it down, Philip, do!' said Dinah. 'Horrid creature!'

'It isn't,' said Philip. 'Look at its dear little feet with fingers on. Do look, Dinah.'

Dinah gave a squeal and pushed Philip away. Lucy-Ann and Jack looked at the tiny lizard with interest.

'It's like a very, very small dragon,' said Jack. 'Open your hand and see if it will stay with you, Philip.'

'Of course it will!' said Philip, who always seemed to exercise a strange spell over any creature he picked up. He opened his hand and let the lizard lie on his open palm. It made no attempt to escape at all.

'See? It wants to stay with me,' said Philip. 'And so it shall. What's your name, little thing? Lizzie? Well, of course, I might have known that.'

Lucy-Ann giggled, forgetting her worries for a moment. What a lovely name for a lizard! Lizzie. Just like Philip to think of that.

'I'll see if I can catch a few flies for you, Lizzie,' said Philip, and went to a sunny patch where flies were buzzing. He caught one and held it in finger and thumb over the lizard's head. In a trice the fly was gone, and the lizard blinked with pleasure.

'Now I suppose you'll let the lizard live in your pocket or somewhere about you for ages,' said Dinah in disgust. 'I shan't go near you. If you haven't got a mouse down your neck you've got a toad in your pocket or a baby hedgehog crawling about you, or a few beetles. I think you're an awful boy.'

'Don't let's squabble now,' said Jack. 'We've bigger things to bother about than lizards.'

The lizard popped into Philip's sleeve. Kiki had been watching it with her head on one side. She was not fond of Philip's pets, and was often jealous of them.

'Pop goes the lizard,' she said, making one of her unexpected apt remarks. The others roared with laughter. Kiki was pleased. She swayed herself from side to side and cracked her beak.

'Shhhhhhhhhh!' she said.

'Oh, Kiki, I'm glad we brought you,' said Jack. 'Now, everybody, what are our next plans?'

'Well, we simply must do a bit of exploring and see if there is anyone living in this valley,' said Philip. 'If there is, we're all right. If there isn't – well, it's just too bad. We'll have to stay here till we're rescued.'

'Rescued! And how do you think anyone is going to rescue us if they haven't the foggiest idea where we are?' demanded Dinah. 'Don't be silly, Philip.'

'Well, do you propose to live here in this valley for the rest of your life, then?' said Philip. 'Oh, here's Lizzie again – coming out of my other sleeve. Lizzie, you're a jolly good explorer, I must say. I wish you could tell us the way out of this valley.'

Dinah went as far from Philip as she could. She simply could not bear his pets. It was a pity, because they were really amusing and friendly.

'You know, we'll have to be careful we don't get lost,' said Lucy-Ann anxiously. 'This valley and these mountainsides are so enormous. We must keep together always.'

'Yes, we must,' agreed Jack. 'And we must always be able to get back to this shed too, because our things are here. At least we shall have shelter here, and our rugs to lie on. If only we had plenty to eat! Those biscuits and chocolate won't last long.'

'Your compass will come in jolly useful, Jack,' said Philip, remembering it. 'Look here – what about setting off now, and doing some more exploring, making this shed a kind of headquarters to come back to?'

'Yes, we will,' said Dinah. 'But let's cover up the suitcases and things with something in case those men come here and see them.'

'They won't,' said Philip. 'What could they possibly want to come snooping round an old burnt cowshed for? We can leave the things here all night.'

They went out of the shed. The sun was just over the mountaintops now, shining into the valley. The children saw the spire of smoke rising straight up from the fire the men must have made.

'So long as we keep away from that direction, we

should be all right,' said Jack. 'Come on – let's take this path. It really looks as if it was once a proper path from this place to somewhere else. We'd better notch the trees here and there as we go, to make sure we find our way back.'

Lucy-Ann liked the idea of that. It reminded her of pioneers and trackers and their ways. Jack and Philip each took out his knife. They made a cut on every fifth tree until they came out of the little wood and found themselves on a flower-strewn, grassy hillside.

'It's lovely, isn't it?' said Lucy-Ann, looking round at the carpet of flowers. 'I've never seen such bright colours. Look at that blue flower, Jack – it's bluer than the sky itself. And oh, look at this tiny pink flower – masses of it!'

'Shall we be seen out on this bare place?' asked Dinah suddenly. Jack and Philip looked downwards into the valley. They had been climbing up, and were now on the mountainside.

'There's the plane!' said Jack. 'And look out – isn't that one of the men walking over to it? Lie down flat, all of you!'

They all promptly lay down flat. Jack had his field glasses on and he put them to his eyes. He could now see clearly that the man was the one called Juan. He had a dead white face, black, thick, curly hair and a small black moustache. His neck was thick and his body was thick too. He disappeared into the plane.

'He's got into the plane. Wonder if he's going off?' said Jack. 'Will he leave the other man behind? He hasn't started up the engines yet.'

After a minute or two the man came out again, carrying something, though Jack could not see what it was. He walked off in the direction of the smoke. There was a thicket of trees near by and he disappeared into this.

'He just went into the plane to get something,' said Jack. 'Now he's gone again. I think perhaps we'd better go another way, because if we can see *him* he could certainly see *us*, if he looked up. See that gully over there? We'll go that way. We shall be well hidden there.'

They made their way to the gully, which was a regular suntrap. There had obviously been a way up there at some time or other. The children followed it, climbing higher. They came to a ledge that ran dangerously round part of the mountainside. Jack went first.

It wasn't as dangerous as it looked. 'I think it's all right,' he called. 'It's wider than it appears. Come on. I'm sure it leads to somewhere.'

They made their way round the ledge, and came to where the hillside gave them a marvellous view down into the valley and all around.

It was completely deserted. Not a cow or sheep or goat to be seen. A little higher up was a black, charred building that had clearly been a very large farm-house. Only the blackened beams were left, and part of the stone walls. Everything else had fallen to the ground and lay in a miserable ugly ruin.

'Another ruin!' said Jack, in awe. 'What *has* been happening in this beautiful valley? I simply can't understand it. Why should houses be burnt like this? I'm beginning to think there isn't a soul here besides ourselves and those two men.'

'I think you're right,' said Philip. 'There's no smoke to be seen anywhere, and not a single domestic animal, not even a dog. But what I can't make out is why no one has come here from the surrounding valleys to rebuild the houses and graze their cattle on this marvellous grass.'

'Perhaps there's something bad about this valley,' said Lucy-Ann with a shiver. 'I don't like the feel of it very much.'

They sat down in the sun, which was now climbing high. They suddenly felt terribly hungry. Dinah unexpectedly produced biscuits and chocolate from a bag she carried.

'I guessed we'd all be hungry soon,' she said. 'So I brought half the biscuits and choc we had with us.'

'Jolly good idea,' said Philip, pleased. 'Hey, Lizzie, come out and have a crumb!'

Dinah at once went a good distance away. Lizzie came out from Philip's open collar and ran down his front. It was plain that she meant to stay with Philip.

'Lizzie's down the well,' remarked Kiki, pecking a piece of chocolate from Jack's fingers.

'Kiki! Give that back!' cried Jack. 'Where are your manners?'

'Down the well, down the well,' said Kiki, who seemed to have got the well on her brain.

They were all thirsty after the chocolate and biscuits. 'I wish we could find something to drink – nice cool clear water like we found in the spring,' said Jack.

'Down the well,' said Kiki.

'All right. You find us a well of water,' said Jack.

'Would it be safe to have a snooze?' asked Dinah, suddenly feeling very sleepy. 'It's nice here in the sun.'

'Well – only just a little one,' said Philip. 'I should think we're safe enough here. Those men wouldn't come up as far as this.'

'You know – I think I can hear water somewhere,' said Lucy-Ann as she lay flat on her back, the sun shining on her freckled face. 'Not very near. Listen, all of you.'

They listened. Certainly they could hear something that was not the wind blowing round. What could it be? It didn't sound like the gurgling of a spring.

'We'll go and see,' said Jack. 'You stay here, girls, if you like. Philip and I will go.'

'Oh, no,' said Lucy-Ann at once. 'I'd rather come with you. You might lose us.'

So all four went off together in the direction of the curious noise. They climbed higher, and came to a rocky, stony part which was steep and hard to climb. But the noise was now much louder.

'Once we round the next corner, we'll see what it is,' said Jack. 'Come on!'

They climbed a little higher and then the path led abruptly round a crag of rock. It widened out a little the other side, and all four children stood gazing in awe at what was making the noise they had heard. It was a waterfall – but what a big one! It fell from a great height, almost sheerly down the mountainside, and cascaded far below them, fine spray rising high in the air. It wetted their faces as they stood there, and yet they were quite a good way from the mass of water.

'What a wonderful sight!' said Philip, awed. 'I've never seen such a big waterfall in my life. What a noise it makes. I almost have to shout. Isn't it grand?'

Far below the waterfall resolved itself into a winding river that curved round the foot of the mountain. The children could not see where it went to. The tumbling water shone and sparkled as it fell, and here and there rainbows shimmered. Lucy-Ann thought she had never seen a lovelier sight.

She licked the spray off her face. It formed into little drops and ran down to her mouth. 'I'm drinking the spray,' she said. 'Oh, look! – there's a puddle in that rock, made of the continually falling spray. Do you think it would be all right to drink it?'

It was very clear and sparkling. Jack tasted it. 'Yes, it's fine,' he said. 'Have some.'

They watched the waterfall for some time. Kiki was simply thrilled with it. For some reason or other it filled her with mad delight. She flew near to it, getting splashed with the drops, squawking loudly.

'It's a magnificent sight!' said Dinah, gazing at the roaring waterfall. 'I could watch it all day.'

'We'll come again tomorrow,' said Jack. 'But I really think we ought to be getting back now to that cowshed. Come on – it's plain there's nobody to help us just here.'

6

What are the two men up to?

Lucy-Ann was half afraid they might lose their way going back. But the boys had taken good note of everything. It was when they got to the wood that difficulty might have arisen, but here the notched trees soon set them right.

They saw that the plane was still down in the valley. So the men were somewhere about. It would be as well to be careful, and Jack told Kiki to be quiet. The waterfall seemed to have gone to her head, and she had been very noisy coming back, singing and squawking loudly.

'There's our shed,' said Lucy-Ann thankfully. It felt quite like home, coming back to it from that enormous mountainside. 'I hope all our things are safe.'

They went inside. Yes, their things were there, exactly as they had left them. Good!

The sun was now sliding down the sky. It was about tea-time. The children wondered whether to finish the rest of their chocolate and biscuits.

'Better not,' said Jack. 'We'll have them before we go to sleep tonight if we're terribly hungry. Oh – wait a minute – what about the stuff Aunt Allie packed for us? Haven't we still got that? We haven't eaten it?'

'No, of course we haven't,' said Dinah. 'I was saving it up. We've got so little that I thought we'd better not start on that picnic packet yet.'

'But all the sandwiches will be stale,' objected Philip, who was feeling very empty indeed. 'What's the good of that? We might as well eat them whilst they're eatable.'

'Well – we could eat the sandwiches, and leave the cake and the chocolate and biscuits for tomorrow,' said Dinah.

'But first let's get this place ready for us to sleep in tonight. It's filthy.'

'I don't want to sleep here,' said Lucy-Ann. 'I don't like it. Why can't we sleep outside? We've got our macks to lie on, and four rugs – and we can unpack some of our clothes and have them for pillows.'

'But it might pour with rain,' said Dinah.

'I could perhaps rig up some sort of roof,' said Jack, looking round at the ruined shed. 'There's some old posts here – and there's a piece of corrugated iron. If Philip gave me a hand, I could rig up the iron sheet on the old posts.'

The two boys tried to do this, but the sheets of iron was not held safely enough. The girls were terrified it might blow off on to them as they slept.

'If only we could find a cave!' said Lucy-Ann.

'Well, we can't,' said Jack, rather cross that all his efforts with the posts and the iron were of no use. 'Anyway, I don't think it's going to rain. Look at the clear sky. If it does pour, we'll have to get into the stall at the end of the cowshed, that's all.'

Their work with the posts had made them hungrier than ever. Dinah undid the picnic packet and took out sandwiches and huge slices of cake. They ate the sandwiches in silence, enjoying every bite immensely.

'Wonder what those men are doing,' said Jack at last. 'I can't see any smoke rising now. Shall I slip down towards the plane, keeping well hidden, and see if I can see them?'

'Yes,' said Philip. 'You're sure you know your way there and back? Don't get lost for goodness' sake!'

'If I do, I'll get Kiki to do her express-engine screech,' said Jack with a grin. 'Then you'll know where we are all right.'

'Look in that plane if you get a chance, and see if you can spot any food there,' called Dinah. Jack went off with Kiki on his shoulder. Lucy-Ann didn't at all like him going off alone. She wished she could have gone with him, but she knew he wouldn't have let her.

'Let's get our beds ready,' said Dinah, who always liked to be doing something. 'Come on, you two – help to unpack the cases and get out something for pillows – and our macks to lie on.'

Whilst Jack was gone the other three were very busy. Soon they had a cosy-looking bed spread on the grass under a big birch tree. First there were the four macks, to keep the damp out. Then there was one big thick rug for softness. There were four piles of woollies for pillows, and finally the other three rugs for coverings.

'That looks very good,' said Dinah approvingly. 'Pull that rug a little over this way, Lucy-Ann. That's right. Philip, you're to sleep right on the outside. I won't have the lizard crawling over me in the night.'

'Lizzie won't hurt you,' said Philip, taking the lizard out of one of his sleeves. 'Will you, Lizzie? Stroke her, Dinah – she's sweet.'

'*Don't*, Philip!' said Dinah with a squeal, as Philip brought the lizard near to her on his outstretched hand. 'I'll box your ears if you dare to let that lizard touch me!'

'Oh, don't tease her, Tufty,' begged Lucy-Ann. 'Let *me* have Lizzie for a bit. I love her.'

But Lizzie would not go to Lucy-Ann, much to her annoyance. She ran up Philip's sleeve and disappeared. Little bumps appearing here and there in his jersey showed where she was.

Dinah looked up at the sky. It was quite clear. The sun had almost gone, and soon the first stars would prick through the sky. She felt tired and irritable.

So did the others. Their short night and the shock they had had were beginning to make themselves felt.

Lucy-Ann felt that at any moment a violent quarrel might spring up between Dinah and Philip.

So she took Dinah off to the spring with her, and they washed in the cold clear water, and drank. They sat there a little while, enjoying the beauty of the valley and the mountains around.

'They seem to be crowding in on us,' said Lucy-Ann. 'Coming closer.'

'How you do imagine things!' said Dinah. 'Come on – let's get back. Jack should be here soon and I want to hear what he's got to say.'

They went back. Philip had laid himself down on the coats and rugs, and was yawning. 'I was just coming to look for you girls,' he said. 'What a time you've been! Jack isn't back yet. I hope he's all right.'

Lucy-Ann felt scared. She adored her brother. She went to stand on a rock, so that she might see when he came. She turned to the others as soon as she got there.

'He's coming!' she called.'And Kiki's on his shoulder.' She jumped down from the rock and rushed to meet Jack. He grinned at her, and Kiki flew off his shoulder to perch on Lucy-Ann's.

'I was beginning to get worried, Jack,' said Lucy-Ann. 'Did anything happen? Did you see the two men? What were they doing?'

They came up to Dinah and Philip. 'My word, what a fine bed!' said Jack, and he sank down on it. 'This is something like! I'm jolly tired.'

'What happened, Jack?' asked Philip. 'Anything?'

'Not much,' said Jack. 'I got as near to the plane as I could, but I didn't dare to go right up in case I was seen, because, as you know, it's right out in the open. I couldn't see or hear anything of the men at all.'

'Was Kiki good?' asked Lucy-Ann anxiously. 'I kept on thinking she might screech or something and draw attention to you.'

'She was as good as gold,' said Jack, scratching Kiki's poll. 'Weren't you, Kiki? Well, I thought the next thing to do would be to try and find where the men were – where that smoke came from. So, keeping as much to the bushes and trees as I could, I made my way towards the smoke. They must have lighted their fire again, because the smoke rose up quite black and thick.'

'Did you see the men?' asked Dinah.

'I heard their voices first,' said Jack. 'Then I thought it would be a good idea to climb a tree and use my field glasses. So up I shinned and came to the top of a nice little tree. Not far below me, near a tumbledown hut, were the two men, cooking something over a fire they had made.'

'Gracious!' said Lucy-Ann. 'Weren't you scared of being seen?'

'No. The tree hid me all right,' said Jack. 'And I hadn't made a scrap of noise. I got my field glasses and looked through them. The men were studying some kind of map.'

'Whatever for?' said Dinah wonderingly. 'I should think they know this part of the world pretty well or they wouldn't have been able to land so easily.'

'Well, they've come here for *some* reason, haven't they?' said Jack. 'Goodness knows what – but certainly for some definite reason. They must be looking for something or someone – and the map will probably show them what they want to know. I heard one say, "This way – and then up here," as if they were planning some sort of expedition.'

'We could follow them,' said Dinah at once. 'Then we'd know.'

'No, thanks,' said Jack. 'I'm not going mountain climbing behind those men. They look jolly tough. What I say is – let them get off on their expedition – and we'll be able to explore that hut of theirs – and the plane too. We may find something to tell us who they are and what they're after.'

'Yes. Let's do that,' said Lucy-Ann sleepily. 'Perhaps they'll go tomorrow. I hope they do. Jack can watch them with his field glasses – and when they're safely gone we can do a good old snoop round.'

'There's really nothing more to tell,' said Jack with a yawn. 'I couldn't hear any more. The men rolled up the map and talked in low voices. So I shinned down the tree and came back. And here I am.'

'Let's snuggle down and go to sleep,' said Lucy-Ann.

'I simply can't keep my eyes open. We're safe here, aren't we?'

'Perfectly, I should think,' said Jack, lying down contentedly. 'Anyway, Kiki will give us warning if anyone comes near. Good night.'

'Good night,' said the others. Philip added a few words.

'Dinah, don't yell if a spider runs over you, or a rat or a hedgehog. There are sure to be plenty out here.'

Dinah gave a squeal and covered her head up at once. Then there was silence. They were all fast asleep.

7

A wonderful find

Soon the stars filled the sky. An owl hooted, and the wind whispered something in the trees overhead. But the four children did not see the stars nor hear the owl and the wind. They were tired out. They slept solidly, and though Dinah was almost smothered with the rug over her head, she did not wake or move.

Kiki slept too, her head under her wing. She was perched on a branch of the birch tree just over Jack's head. She awoke when she heard the owl, and hooted back softly. Then she put her head back under her wing and slept again.

When dawn came the children were still asleep. Kiki awoke before they did. She stretched out first one wing and then the other. She erected the feathers on her head and shook them. Then she scratched her neck thoughtfully and gazed down at Philip.

Lizzie the lizard was also awake and was running over the rug that covered Philip. She came to where Philip's feet stuck out and disappeared under the rug there. Kiki's sharp eyes watched the little moving bump she made under the rug as she made her way all the way up Philip's body and appeared by his neck.

'Wipe your feet,' said Kiki suddenly to the lizard. 'How many times, how many times have I told you to wipe your feet?'

Lizzie was startled. She leapt from Philip's neck on to Jack and stood half hidden in his hair, looking up into the trees, though she could focus on nothing there. Kiki, annoyed at seeing Lizzie daring to tread on her beloved master, gave an exasperated squawk and flew down to peck the lizard, who promptly disappeared under the rug again.

Kiki landed heavily on Jack's middle and gave a vicious peck where the rug covered Philip's right leg, for she could see the moving bump there that meant the lizard was running downwards. Both Jack and Philip awoke with a start.

They stared up into the trees, amazed to see green leaves waving above them. Then they turned their heads and saw one another. In a flash they remembered everything.

'Couldn't think where I was,' said Jack, and sat up. 'Oh, Kiki, it's you on my middle, is it? Do get off. Here, have some sunflower seeds and keep quiet, or you'll wake the girls.'

He put his hand in his pocket and took out some of

the flat seeds that Kiki loved. She flew up to the bough above, cracking two in her beak.

The boys began to talk quietly, so as not to disturb the girls, who were still sleeping peacefully.

'Gosh, I feel better now,' said Jack, stretching out his arms. 'I was so tired last night I could have cried. What about you, Philip?'

'I'm all right too,' said Philip, and he yawned hugely. 'But sleepy still. Well, we haven't got to get up for breakfast. We shan't hear any gong sounding here. Let's have another snooze.'

But Jack was now too wide awake to snooze. He slipped out from under the rug and went to wash himself at the spring. He gazed downwards and saw the spire of smoke rising up just as it had yesterday.

'Those fellows are up and about,' he said to himself. 'Must be getting late in the morning, I suppose. The sun's fairly high. Blow! I forgot to wind up my watch last night.'

Soon the girls woke up and were amazed to find they had slept soundly all the night through and had apparently not even stirred. Dinah looked to see where Lizzie was.

'It's all right,' said Philip amiably. 'She's down one of my socks. I like the feel of her tiny fingers on my leg.'

'Ugh! You're awful!' said Dinah. 'Well, I'm going to wash. Then we'll have breakfast – only cake and biscuits, I'm afraid.'

Unfortunately they were all so hungry that they devoured the cake, the biscuits and the rest of the chocolate too. Now there was no food left at all.

'We'll just *have* to do something about it – about the food question, I mean,' said Dinah. 'Even if it means eating your lizard, Philip.'

'She wouldn't make more than a mouthful, would you, Liz?' said Philip. 'Hallo – what's that?'

'That' was the sound of voices. Hurriedly the four children got up, and, dragging their rugs, macks and other clothes with them, they ran quickly to the cowshed. They dumped the things into the last stall and crouched there, panting.

'Have we left anything at all out there?' whispered Jack.

'Don't think so,' whispered back Philip. 'The grass is a bit flattened, that's all. Let's hope they won't notice it.'

There was a crack in the side of the old cowshed and Jack put his eye to it. They had only just got away in time. The men were coming slowly up towards the birch trees, talking. They came to where the children had slept the night before.

The men walked right past the spot, then one of them stopped and looked back with a puzzled expression. He gazed at the place where the children had slept. What he said they couldn't hear, but he pointed to the flattened grass. Both men then walked back and looked earnestly down at it.

'What's done that?' asked the man called Juan.

'Funny,' said the other man. He had a large pink face with full lips, and his eyes looked small in comparison. 'Some animal, perhaps?'

'Why – that's big enough for an elephant or two to lie on!' said Juan. 'Shall we have a look round?'

The other man looked at his watch. 'No. Not now,' he said. 'When we come back, perhaps. We've got a lot to do today. Come on. It can't be anything really.'

They went on again and were soon lost to sight among the trees. 'I'm going to get up a tree with my field glasses and follow them with them as they go,' said Jack to the others. 'We must make certain they really are gone before we show ourselves.'

He went cautiously out of the shed and ran quickly to a tall tree. He was up it in a trice, for he was an excellent climber. He sat at the top, balanced on a swaying branch, his legs wound tightly round it. He put his glasses to his eyes.

As soon as the men came out on to the grassy, flowery part of the hillside he saw them. They did not take the same direction as the children had taken the day before, but kept on the flowery part for a long time. Jack could see them easily with his glasses. Then they took out a map or paper and stood there looking at it between them.

'Not sure of their way,' thought the boy. 'Ah – now they're off again.'

The men began to climb steeply and Jack watched them as long as he could see them. Then they rounded a great crag of rock and disappeared from sight. He slid down the tree.

'Gracious! We thought you'd gone to sleep in the tree,' said Dinah impatiently. 'I'm tired of waiting in this filthy shed. Have the men gone?'

'Yes. They're far away now,' said Jack. 'It's quite safe to come out and have a look round. They didn't go the way we did. I watched them climbing very steeply up the mountainside. Come on – let's get off whilst we can.'

'We could go and have a look inside the aeroplane now,' said Dinah. So they all hurried down to the valley, and came to where the big aeroplane stood on its enormous wheels. The four children climbed up the steps into the cockpit.

'The big crate's gone,' said Jack at once. 'I wonder how they got it out. It must have been empty or they could never have managed it between them. Look – there's where we hid the other night!'

Philip and Jack hunted all round the plane for food or information. But there was no food at all, and not a scrap of paper that would give them any idea as to who the men were or why they had come there.

They all climbed out again. 'Blow!' said Jack. 'We're no better off now! Not even a bar of chocolate. We shall starve!'

'If we could explore that hut you saw the men by last

night, I bet we'd find plenty of food,' said Dinah. 'Don't you remember the men saying, "Let's go to the hut and have a meal"? Well, they couldn't have a meal without food, could they? – so the food must be there.'

This was a distinctly cheering idea. Jack led the way to where he had seen the men sitting by the campfire the night before. The fire was almost out, though it was still smouldering a little.

The hut lay near by. It was tumbledown, but not burnt as had been all the other buildings they had seen. Rough repairs had been done to it. The one window looked strong, and was hardly big enough for anyone to get in or out, if he had wanted to. The door was also a strong one. It was shut.

'Locked, of course,' said Jack, giving it a tug. '*And* they've taken the key. Who did they imagine was going to come along and take anything? They don't know a thing about *us*.'

'Let's look in at the window,' said Lucy-Ann. 'We could see inside easily.'

Jack hoisted Philip up. The boy looked inside, finding it difficult at first to make out anything, because the interior of the shed was dark. The only light came in from the small window.

'Ah – now I can see better,' said Philip. 'There are a couple of mattresses – and rugs – and a table and some chairs – and a stove of some kind. And gosh – just look at *that*!'

'What?' cried everyone impatiently. Lucy-Ann jumped up and down, trying to see in at the window too.

'*Stacks* of food!' said Philip. 'Tins and tins of it! And pots and jars of stuff! Golly, they make my mouth water.'

Jack could bear Philip's weight no longer. He set him down with a jerk.

'Hoist *me* up, now,' he said, and Philip gave him a hoist. Jack's eyes nearly fell out of his head when he saw the food, neatly piled on shelves that ran along one side of the hut.

'It's a kind of storehouse, or resthouse,' he said, jumping down from Philip's back. 'My word, if we could only get some! Why did those men take the key? Distrustful creatures!'

'Can we get in at the window?' asked Philip, and he looked eagerly up at it. 'No, we can't. Not even Lucy-Ann could get in there. Besides, it can't be opened. It's just a pane of glass set into the window frame, with no catch or fastener to open it. We'd have to smash it – and that would give away the fact that somebody was here.'

The children wandered gloomily round the shed. Then they set off to see if there was anything else to be found near by. But there wasn't.

'I suppose we'd better get back to our own shed and remove our things, and hide them somewhere else in case those men do have a look round when they come back,' said Jack. 'How I hate leaving all that food in this shed! I'm starving.'

'So am I,' said Lucy-Ann. 'I could almost eat Kiki's sunflower seeds.'

'Well, have some,' said Jack, holding out a handful. 'They're not poisonous.'

'No, thanks,' said Lucy-Ann. 'I'm not as starving as all that.'

Philip went up to the door of the shed and glared at it. 'I'd like to knock you down,' he said. 'Standing there between ourselves and a good square meal. Take that!'

To the great amusement of the others he aimed a hearty kick at the door, and then another.

It flew open. The children gasped in surprise, and stared. 'It wasn't locked, after all!' cried Jack, 'just shut. What idiots we were to think it was locked! Come on – now for a feast!'

8

Kiki talks too much

They all crowded into the dimly lighted shed. They gazed joyfully at the piles of things on the shelves.

'Biscuits! Tongue! Pineapple! Sardines! Milk! Gosh, there's everything here!' cried Jack. 'What shall we start on?'

'Wait a bit. Don't let's disarrange the shelf so much that the men will know someone has been here,' said Philip. 'Better take tins from the back, not the front. And we won't eat the fruit and other stuff here – we'll take it away with us.'

'I think,' said Jack slowly – 'I really do think it would be a good idea to take away as much of this as we can carry, in case we are stuck in this valley for some time. We may as well face the fact that we are completely lost, and cut off from the world we know, and may not be rescued for ages.'

The others looked solemn, and Lucy-Ann looked scared as well.

'You're right, Freckles,' said Philip. 'We'll help ourselves, to as much as we can carry. Look, here's a pile of old sacks. What about filling a couple of them with the tins and carrying them off between us? We could take dozens of the tins then.'

'Good idea,' said Jack. 'Here's a sack for you and Dinah to fill, and here's one for me and Lucy-Ann.'

Philip stood on one of the chairs and reached his hand behind the front row of tins on the shelf. He threw down tin after tin, and the others put them into the two sacks. What a store there was in that hut!

Soon the sacks were full and almost too heavy to carry. It was nice to think of all that food waiting to be eaten. Jack found a tin-opener too, and put it in his pocket.

'Before we go, let's have a look and see if we can find any papers or documents that will tell us something about these mysterious airmen,' said Philip. But although they hunted in every corner, and even under the pile of sacks, they could find nothing.

'I wonder what they did with that crate they had in the plane,' said Jack. 'We haven't found that anywhere. I'd like to have a squint at that too.'

The crate was not in the shed. So the children wandered out and had another good look round. And, in a copse of young trees and bushes, with a tarpaulin over them, they found about six of the wooden crates.

'Funny,' said Jack, pulling away the tarpaulin. 'Look

– lots of them – all empty! What are they going to put into them?'

'Goodness knows!' said Philip. 'Who would bring empty crates to this deserted valley, hoping to find something to fill them? Only madmen!'

'Oh – you don't really think those men are mad, do you?' said Lucy-Ann in alarm. 'What shall we do if they are?'

'Keep out of their way, that's all,' said Philip. 'Come on. Did we shut that door? Yes, we did. Now, heave-ho, Dinah, catch hold of your end of the sack and we'll go back to our shed.'

Stumbling under the weight of the clanking sacks, the four children made their way slowly back to the shed they had hidden their things in. Jack dumped his sack, and then ran to climb the tree he had climbed before, in order to sweep the countryside with his field glasses, and see if the men were by any chance returning yet. But there was no sign of them.

'All clear at the moment,' said Jack, going back to the others. 'Now for a meal – the finest we've ever had because we've never been so hungry before.'

They chose a tin of biscuits and opened it. They took out about forty biscuits, feeling perfectly certain that they could manage at least ten each. They opened a tin of tongue, which Jack carved very neatly with his penknife. Then they opened a tin of pineapple chunks and a tin of milk.

'What a meal!' said Jack, sitting down contentedly on the sun-warmed ground. 'Well – here goes!'

Never did food taste so completely delicious. 'Mmm-mm-mmm,' murmured Lucy-Ann, meaning, 'This is simply gorgeous.' Kiki imitated her at once.

'Mmm-mm-mm! Mmm-mm-mm!'

No word was spoken except when Dinah saw Kiki delving too deeply into the tin of pineapple.

'Jack! Do stop Kiki! She'll eat it all!'

Kiki retired to a branch of the tree above, a large chunk of pineapple in her claw. 'Mmm-mm-mm!' she kept saying. 'Mmm-mm-mm!'

Dinah went to the spring and rinsed out the empty tin of milk. Then she filled it with clear cold water and came back. She emptied the cold water into the pineapple juice left at the bottom of the tin and shook it up. Then she offered everyone a pineapple drink to end the meal.

'Gosh! I do feel better now,' said Jack, and he undid his belt to let it out two or three holes. 'Thank goodness you lost your temper and kicked that door, Philip. We were so sure that it was locked, and the key taken.'

'Silly of us,' said Philip, lying down and shutting his eyes. 'What are we going to do with the empty tins?'

'*You're* obviously going to do nothing,' said Dinah. 'I'll push them down a rabbit hole. The rabbits can lick them out.'

She picked up a tin and gave a scream. She dropped

it, and Lizzie the lizard ran out in a hurry. She had been sniffing in delight at the crumbs of tongue left there. The tiny creature ran to Philip, and disappeared down his neck.

'Don't tickle, Lizzie,' murmured Philip sleepily.

'I'd better keep a watch out in case the men come back,' said Jack, and he climbed his tree again. Lucy-Ann and Dinah stuffed the empty tins down a large rabbit hole.

Kiki looked down the hole at the tins in surprise, then walked solemnly down and began to tug at one of the tins.

'No, Kiki, don't!' said Lucy-Ann. 'Jack, take Kiki with you up the tree.'

Jack whistled. Kiki flew to him at once and perched on his shoulder as he climbed his tree, moving from side to side when a bough threatened to knock her off.

'We'd better bring out all our cases and things, ready to hide them somewhere better than in the cowshed,' said Dinah. 'If those men do look round here when they come back, they'll see them in the cowstall, as sure as anything!'

So the two girls lugged everything out, Dinah grumbling because Philip lay apparently asleep and would not stir himself to help them. Jack came down the tree.

'No sign of them yet,' he said. 'Now the thing is – where can we hide these things really well?'

'Down the well,' suggested Kiki, hearing the word 'well.'

'Shut up, Kiki,' said Jack. He looked all round but could think of nowhere. Then an idea struck him.

'I'll tell you where would be a jolly good place,' he said.

'Where?' asked the girls.

'Well – see that big tree there? – the one with thick spreading branches – we could get up there and pull up our things quite easily, and hide them in the leafy branches. No one would think of looking up there, either for us or our belongings.'

The girls gazed at the thickly leafed tree. It was a horse-chestnut tree, dark and full of glossy leaves. Just the place.

'But how can we get the suitcases up?' asked Dinah. 'They're not terribly big – but they're quite heavy.'

Jack undid a rope from round his waist. He nearly always had one there. 'Here you are!' he said. 'I can climb up the tree and let down this rope. You can slip it through the handle of one of the suitcases and knot it. Then I'll give a jolly good heave – and up it'll come!'

'Let's wake Philip, then,' said Dinah, who didn't see why her brother shouldn't join in the labour of heaving things up a tree. She went over and shook him. He awoke with a jump.

'Come and help us, you lazy thing,' said Dinah. 'Jack's found a marvellous hiding place for us all.'

Philip joined the others and agreed that it was indeed a fine place. He said he would go up with Jack and pull up the cases.

Kiki was most interested in all the proceedings. When Jack hung the rope down the tree, she flew to it and gave it such a tug with her beak that it was pulled from Jack's hand and fell to the ground.

'Kiki! What did you do that for, you bad bird?' called Jack. 'Now I've got to climb all the way down and up again! Idiot!'

Kiki went off into one of her neverending cackles of laughter. She waited her chance and once again pulled the rope from poor Jack's hand.

Jack called her sternly. She came, cracking her beak, not quite liking Jack's stern voice. He tapped her very sharply on the beak.

'Bad Kiki! Naughty Kiki! Go away! I don't want you. No, GO AWAY!'

Kiki flew off, squawking dismally. Jack was not very often cross with her, but she knew he was this time. She retired inside the dark cowshed, and sat high up on a blackened beam, swaying herself to and fro.

'Poor Kiki! Poor, poor Kiki!' she groaned. 'Pop goes Kiki!'

Jack and Philip soon hauled everything up and stowed it safely away in the forks of the big spreading branches. Then Jack shinned up a bit higher and put his glasses to his eyes. What he saw made him call urgently to the girls.

'The men are coming! Quick, get up! Have you left anything behind? Have a look and see!'

The girls took a quick look round. They could see nothing. Lucy-Ann climbed the tree quickly, with Dinah just behind her. They settled themselves on broad branches and peered down. They could see nothing at all, for the leaves were far too thick. Well, if they couldn't see down, certainly nobody could see up. So that was all right.

Soon they could hear voices. The men were coming near. The children sat as quiet as mice in the tree. Lucy-Ann felt a terrible longing to cough and she put her hand over her mouth.

Down below, the men were making a good search of the old cowshed. They found nothing, of course, for everything had been removed by the children. Then they wandered out again and looked at the flattened grass. It puzzled them very much.

'I'll just have one more look in that shed,' said the man called Juan. He disappeared into the shed once more. Kiki, who was still up on the blackened beam, sulking, was annoyed to see him again.

'Wipe your feet,' she said severely. 'And how many times have I told you to shut the door?'

The man jumped violently and peered all round. Kiki was huddled in a corner up in the roof and he could not see her. He looked in all the other corners of the room, hardly believing his ears. He called to his companion.

'Look here,' he said, 'somebody just now told me to wipe my feet and shut the door.'

'You're mad,' said the other man. 'You can't be feeling well.'

'Pussy down the well,' announced Kiki. 'Well, well, well! Use your handkerchief.'

The men clutched one another. Kiki's voice was so unexpected in that dark shed.

'Let's be quiet and listen,' said Juan. Kiki heard the words 'be quiet.'

'Shhhhhhhhhshhhhhhh!' she said at the top of her voice. That was too much for the men. They fled out into the open air.

9

New plans

Kiki was glad to see the two men go. 'Shut the door!' she shouted after them. 'Shut the door!'

The men ran off, and only stopped when they were well away from the shed. Juan mopped his forehead.

'What do you make of *that*?' he said. 'A voice – and nothing else!'

The other man was rapidly recovering.

'Where there's a voice there's a body,' he said. 'There's somebody here – somebody playing tricks on us. I thought when I saw that flattened piece this morning that we were not alone here. Who's here? Do you think anybody's got wind of the treasure?'

The four children, hidden well in the leaves of the tree, just above the heads of the two men, pricked up their ears at once. Treasure! Oho! So that was what the men were after in this lonely, deserted valley. Treasure!

'How could anyone know what we know?' said Juan

scornfully. 'Don't get nerves just because you heard a voice, Pepi. Why, maybe it was just a parrot.'

Pepi laughed loudly. It was his turn to be scornful now. 'A parrot! What will you say next, Juan?' he said with a sneer.

'Have you ever known parrots to live here before? And talking ones too? If that's a parrot, I'll eat my hat and yours as well!'

The listening children grinned at one another. Lucy-Ann thought she would like to see Pepi, whoever he was, eating his hat. He would have to eat Juan's too, for Kiki was most certainly a parrot.

'It's somebody hiding about here,' said Pepi. 'Though how they got here goodness knows. Juan, maybe there is a cellar beneath that cowshed. We will go and find out if anyone is hiding there. He will be very – very – sorry for himself.'

The children didn't like the tone of his voice at all. Lucy-Ann shivered. What horrid men!

They went cautiously to the cowshed. Juan stood at the broken-down doorway. He called loudly: 'Come out of the cellar, whoever you are! We give you this one chance!'

No one came out, of course. For one thing there was no one to come out, and for another there was no cellar to come from. Juan held a revolver in his hand. Kiki, rather alarmed at the shouting voice, said nothing at all, which was fortunate for her.

The silence was too much for Juan. He took aim at where he supposed a cellar might be and a shot rang out. BANG!

Kiki almost tumbled off the beam in fright and the four children nearly fell out of their tree. Jack just clutched Lucy-Ann in time and held her tightly.

BANG! Another shot. The children imagined that Juan must be firing blindly, merely to frighten the person he thought he had heard talking. What a pity Kiki had been in the shed, sulking. Jack felt most alarmed. He was afraid she might have been shot.

The men came out again. They stood looking about for some moments and then walked near to the chestnut tree, talking.

'No one there now. Must have slipped off. I tell you, Pepi, there has been someone here – maybe spying on us!'

'Well, he surely wouldn't give himself away by telling us to wipe our feet and shut the door,' said Pepi scornfully.

'We'll come back tomorrow and search this place completely,' said Juan. 'I'm certain there's somebody here. Talking English too! What does it mean? I feel very alarmed about it. We didn't want anyone to get wind of our mission.'

'Certainly we must search this place well,' said Pepi. 'We must find out who is the owner of that voice. No doubt about that. I'd start a good hunt now, but it's getting dark and I'm hungry. Come on – let's get back.'

To the children's huge relief the men disappeared. Jack, who by climbing to the very top of the tree could see the aeroplane, waited till he could see the two men passing by it on their way to their own hut.

Then he called down to the others, 'All clear now. They're by the plane. My word – what a shock I had when those shots went off! Lucy-Ann nearly fell off her branch.'

'Lizzie shot out of my pocket and disappeared,' said Philip. 'I say, I hope Kiki's all right, Jack. She must have been scared out of her life when the shots rang out in that little shed.'

Kiki was sitting petrified on the beam when the children went into the cowshed. She crouched down, trembling. Jack called to her softly.

'It's all right, Kiki. Come on down. I'm here to fetch you.'

Kiki flew down at once and landed on Jack's shoulder. She made a great fuss of him. 'Mmm-mm-mm!' she kept saying. 'Mmm-mm-mm!'

It was dark in the shed. The children didn't like it. Lucy-Ann kept feeling there might be someone hiding in the corners. 'Let's go out,' she said. 'What are we going to do tonight? Is it safe to sleep where we did last night?'

'No. We'd better take our rugs and things somewhere else,' said Jack. 'There's a patch of bushes higher up where we'd be sheltered from the wind and hidden from view too. We could take them there.'

'I say – do you know what we left in the shed?' said Philip suddenly. 'We left our sacks of tins. Look, there they are in that corner.'

'What a mercy the men didn't notice they were full of something!' said Jack. 'Still, I'm not surprised they took no notice of them really. They just look like heaps of rubbish. We'll drag them up to the bushes, though. Our store of food is too precious to be left behind.'

They dragged the sacks to the patch of bushes and left them there. Then they debated what to do about the things up the tree.

'Let's just bring down the rugs and our macks,' said Jack. 'The clothes we used for pillows are wrapped in the rugs. We could leave the suitcases up there. We don't want to drag them about with us.'

It was now getting so dark that it was quite difficult to get the rugs and macks down, but they managed it somehow. Then they made their way again to the bushes. Dinah and Lucy-Ann spread out the 'bed,' as they called it.

'It won't be so warm here,' said Dinah. 'The wind creeps round rather. Where are we going to hide tomorrow? Those men will look behind these bushes, that's certain.'

'Do you remember that waterful?' asked Philip. 'There seemed to be a nice lot of rocks and hiding places down towards the foot. I believe we could climb down there and find quite a good place.'

'Yes, let's,' said Lucy-Ann. 'I'd like to see that water-fall again.'

They all lay down on the rug. They pressed close together, for it was certainly cold. Dinah took a pullover from her 'pillow' and put it on.

Suddenly she gave a scream, making the others jump. 'Oh! Oh! There's something running over me! It must be a rat!'

'Well, it isn't,' came Philip's delighted voice. 'It's Lizzie! She's found me. Good old Lizzie!'

So it was. How the little lizard had discovered where Philip was nobody could imagine. It was part of the spell that Philip always seemed to exercise on wild creatures.

'Don't worry, Dinah,' said Philip. 'Lizzie is safe in my pocket now. Poor thing. I bet she felt dizzy falling down the tree.'

'Dizzy Lizzie,' said Kiki at once, delighted with the two words. 'Dizzy Lizzie.'

Everyone laughed. Kiki was really funny at times. 'Doesn't she love to put words together that have the same sounds?' said Lucy-Ann. 'Do you remember last hols she kept saying "Fusty-musty-dusty" till we nearly screamed at her?'

'Fusty-musty-dusty, dizzy Lizzie,' said Kiki at once, and screeched.

'Don't,' said Jack. 'You're only showing off now, Kiki.

Go to sleep. And if you dig your claws into my tummy like you did this morning, I'll smack you.'

'God save the Queen,' said Kiki devoutly, and said no more.

The children talked for a little while longer. Then the girls and Philip fell asleep. Jack lay on his back, with Kiki on one of his ankles. He looked up at the stars. What was the good of promising Aunt Allie they wouldn't have any more adventures? The very night they had promised her, they had whizzed off in a strange aeroplane to an unknown valley, where, apparently, some sort of 'treasure' was hidden. Most extraordinary. Most – extra – And then Jack was asleep too, and the stars shone down on the four children, moving across the sky till dawn slid into the east and put out all the stars one by one.

Philip awoke early. He had meant to, for he did not know how early the men might start hunting for the owner of the 'voice'. He awoke the others and would not listen to their protests.

'No, you've really got to wake up, Dinah,' he said. 'We must start early today. Go on – wake up! – or I'll put Dizzy Lizzie down your neck.'

That woke poor Dinah up properly. She sat up and tried to slap Philip, but he dodged away. She hit Kiki instead. The parrot gave a surprised and aggrieved squawk.

'Oh, *sorry*, Kiki,' said Dinah. 'Sorry. I didn't mean that for you. Poor, poor Kiki!'

'What a pity, what a pity!' said Kiki, flying off in case Dinah sent out any more slaps.

'We'll have a quick breakfast,' said Jack. 'Sardines, biscuits and milk, I think. I saw a tin of sardines at the top of one of our sacks. Yes, here it is.'

They saw smoke rising up from where the two men were, and knew that they too were up. So they finished their breakfast quickly, and Dinah once more pushed the tins down a convenient rabbit hole. Then they ruffled up the grass on which they had been lying, so that it didn't look quite so flat.

'I think we'd better find a good hiding place for most of these tins,' said Philip, 'and take just a few of them with us to last us for today. We can't possibly lug these heavy sacks along all the way.'

'Couldn't we drop them into the middle of these bushes?' said Dinah. 'They're awfully thick. Nobody would guess they were there. We could slip back and fetch any we wanted.'

So the sacks were dropped into the middle of the bushes, and certainly no one could see them unless they actually crawled into the very middle. Then the children gathered up their rugs, macks and odd clothes and set off. The boys carried the tins, and Jack had his camera and his glasses as well. So they were heavily laden and could not go very fast.

They took the same way that they had taken before. When they came to the grassy, flower-strewn hillside they sat down for a rest. After all, the men would hardly be following them! They would be hunting all round and about the cowshed.

Suddenly, from far off, Jack caught sight of a brilliant, twinkling flash. He lay down flat at once, telling the others to do the same. 'There's someone using field-glasses down there,' he said. 'We may not be seen if we lie flat. I just caught the flash of the sun on the eye-lenses. Dash! I forgot the men might sweep the mountainside with glasses. They'll be after us if they've seen us.'

'Let's crawl to that rock and get behind it,' said Philip. 'Come on. Once we're behind there we can get on and find the waterfall.'

10

A fine hiding-place

When they were behind the rock the children felt sure they could not be seen, and they breathed more easily. Philip looked round and about. The gully they had been in before lay a little to the left. They could reach it without being seen from below.

'Come on,' said Philip, choosing a path that put rocks or bushes between them and the valley below. 'This way.'

Up the hot gully went the children, and came to the ledge that ran round a steep bit of the mountain. They made their way round and once more saw the wonderful view they had seen before. Above them stood the ruined, burnt-out farmhouse. Lucy-Ann carefully didn't look at it. It gave her such a miserable feeling to see the blackened beams and fallen walls.

They stood and listened for the sound of the waterfall. It came softly to their ears, a continous, musical sound, like a far-off orchestra playing a simple tune.

'What a lovely noise!' said Dinah. 'Philip, shall we

climb down or up now? If you want to go to the foot of the waterfall and hide somewhere among the rocks there, we ought to climb down, oughtn't we? Last time we climbed up – over that rocky, stony bit.'

The boys stood and considered. 'It would perhaps be best if we went down this time,' said Jack at last. 'Those rocks just above the waterfall may be slippery to climb down on, for they will be wet with the spray. We don't want to slip, and we're carrying so many things that we haven't free hands to use.'

So they chose a way that led downwards. Philip went first, finding the safest path he could; not that there was a real path, of course, for there was not. As they came near to the waterfall, spray blew around them, and left a fine wet mist on their hair. They were hot with climbing and the spray was deliciously cool.

They rounded a corner, and saw the whole of the cascading water at once. What a sight! Lucy-Ann drew a quick breath of awe and delight, and stood staring.

'What a thunderous noise!' shouted Jack, trying to make his voice heard. 'It makes me feel all excited.'

'It does me too,' agreed Dinah. 'As if I want to do a jig or a hornpipe or something. And it makes me want to shout and yell.'

'Well, let's!' said Jack, and he began to caper and shout as if he was mad. The others did the same, except Lucy-Ann. It was almost as if they were trying to out-shout and outdance the tumbling, roaring water.

They soon stopped, quite exhausted. They were on a flat rock which was wet with the flying spray. They were not nearly at the foot of the water after all, but about a quarter of the way up the fall. The noise filled their ears, and sometimes the force of the spray made them gasp. It was somehow very exciting.

'Well,' said Jack at last, when they had gazed their fill at the waterfall, 'let's think about a good hiding place. I must say I don't think those men would dream of coming here to look for us.'

They all looked about for a cave or mass of rocks in or behind which they could hide. Lucy-Ann looked a little doubtful.

'I don't know if I can bear to hear this terrific noise going on in my ears all the time,' she called to Jack. 'It makes me feel a bit dizzy.'

'Dizzy Lizzie,' remarked Kiki at once. She too had been excited by the waterfall and had shouted with the others.

'Well, you'll have to put up with the noise,' said Jack. 'You'll soon get used to it.'

Lucy-Ann looked worried. She was quite sure she wouldn't get used to that thundering going on all the time. She would never, never be able to sleep through it.

The children wandered about by the waterfall, not going too near it because of the thick spray around it. They couldn't seem to find any good place to hide in at all. All the rocks there seemed to be wet, and there seemed to be no comfortable spot in which to put their things.

'Our rugs would be soaked in no time with the fine mist that hangs about the fall,' said Dinah. 'And we can't possibly lie on wet rugs. I don't believe this is such a good idea after all.'

Jack was climbing a little higher. He came to where a giant fern grew. It hung down like a great green curtain and was lovely to see. Jack wondered whether they could hide behind it.

He pushed aside the hanging green fronds and gave a shout at once. The others didn't hear it because of the noise of the water.

'Golly!' said Jack to himself. 'There's a cave behind this hanging fern – and it will be quite dry because the fern screens it from the spray. It's like a great thick curtain! Hey, you others!'

But again nobody heard him. Jack couldn't wait for them to pay attention to him. He went through the hanging fronds and found himself in a dim dry cave, with a fairly low roof, and moss growing on the floor. He felt it. It was dry. Probably when the fern died down in the autumn, the spray flew into the cave and the moss then grew damp and flourished well. But now it was like a soft, dry green bed.

'This is just – exactly – the place for us,' said Jack, delighted. 'Absolutely marvellous! Nobody could possibly see us here because the fern hangs down over the entrance, and it was only quite by accident I found it. It would be a most exciting place for us.'

There was a ledge running round one side of it, like a bench. 'We could put all our things there – tins and so on,' said Jack to himself. 'And when we've put our macks down on this moss we'll have a most lovely bed. I really *must* tell the others.'

It was quite time that he showed himself, for the others had now missed him and were yelling at the tops of their voices for him.

'Jack! JA-CK! Where are you? JACK!'

Jack heard their voices as he pushed aside the fern fronds and looked out, just his head showing. Dinah and Kiki suddenly caught sight of his face peering out of the fern some way above them. Kiki gave a squawk of surprise and flew up at once. Dinah jumped.

'Look!' she yelled to Philip and Lucy-Ann. 'Look where Jack is – hiding behind that giant fern!'

Jack put his hands to his mouth and yelled at the top of his voice, trying to drown the noise of the waterfall. 'Come on up here! I've found something marvellous!'

The others climbed up eagerly. Jack held aside the green fronds for them. 'Won't you come into my parlour!' he said politely. '*So* pleased to see you all.'

They passed through the green curtain into the cave behind. They called out in delighted surprise.

'What a lovely place! Nobody could ever find us here!'

'There's a soft green carpet on the floor! It's moss!'

'The roar of the fall isn't nearly so loud here! We can hear ourselves speak!'

'Glad you like it,' said Jack modestly. 'I found it quite by accident. It's perfect, isn't it?'

It was. Lucy-Ann was relieved that the thunder of the waterfall was lessened here, in the cave. Dinah was thrilled with the softness of the moss. Philip was pleased by the real safety of such a hiding place. Nobody would ever find it except by chance.

'Let's go and fetch our things from the rock where we left them,' said Dinah, who always liked all her belongings set out neatly together. 'There is plenty of room for them here. I shall put our tins of food on that rocky ledge.'

'We can only *just* stand upright,' said Philip. He went to where the green fronds hung down over the entrance, making the cave rather dark. He parted the fronds and at once a ray of sunshine fell into the cave, lighting it up well.

'We could tie back some of the fern so that we get the sun in the cave,' said Philip. 'We've got a jolly good view of the waterfall from here – and we can see everything around well, so that if anyone comes we shall spot them at once. It's fine.'

'I shan't mind living here a bit for a little while,' said Lucy-Ann happily. 'I feel safe here.'

'You may have to live here a *long* while,' said Philip. 'Well – I can think of worse places.'

'Those men would never find us here,' said Jack. 'Never!'

He tied back some of the fronds, and the children sat down on the floor for a little while, enjoying the sunshine that now poured in. The moss was like a cushion to sit on.

After a bit they all climbed down to where they had left their rugs and tins and other things. They carried them up to their new home. Dinah arranged the loose things on the rocky ledge. They looked nice there.

'We shall have a lovely soft bed tonight,' she said. 'We ought to sleep jolly well in here. It's not musty or stuffy.'

'Fusty-musty-dusty,' said Kiki at once, remembering the three words she had learnt in the last holidays. 'Fusty-musty-dusty, fusty . . .'

'Oh, don't begin that again, Kiki,' said Jack. 'We got tired of that long ago.'

Kiki flew to his shoulder, and looked out of the strange little cave. There was really a wonderful view outside – first of all, the cascading waterfall, with rainbows caught in it here and there; then beyond it the steep mountainside, and far beyond that, lower down, the green valley which stretched to the foot of steep mountains on the opposite side, towering up one behind the other.

It was about time for a meal again. All the children seemed to get hungry at the same time, and they glanced at the tins on the shelf or ledge. Jack felt for his tin-opener.

'You mind you don't lose it,' said Philip. 'That's our most precious possession at the moment, Jack – your tin-opener.'

'Don't worry. I shan't lose it,' said Jack, and began to open a tin. Kiki watched with her head on one side. She liked these tins. They had most exciting things inside, she considered.

Soon they were sitting eating hungrily, looking out of the cave entrance to the sparkling waterfall not far off. It was nice to sit there munching away, with that lovely view outside, the soft moss beneath them and the warm sun on their bare legs.

'We do seem to have some adventures,' said Jack. 'It's most peculiar the way we can't seem to keep out of them. I do hope Bill and Aunt Allie aren't worrying too much about us. If only we could get word to them!'

'We can't,' said Philip. 'We're stuck here all alone, with no means of getting into touch with anyone as far as I can see – except those two men. I'm blessed if I know what to do. Thank goodness we've got plenty of food.'

'We'd better go back to that bush where we dumped the rest of the tins and fetch them along here as soon as we can,' said Jack. 'What we've brought won't last us more than today. Will you two girls be all right if Philip and I go along and get what we can? We shan't be able to bring them all at one go. We must make several journeys.'

'Yes, we shall be quite all right here,' said Dinah, giving Kiki the last bit of salmon out of her tin. 'You set off this afternoon. You can leave Kiki here to guard us.'

11

The cave of echoes

It was very early in the afternoon. The boys knew they would have plenty of time to go to the bush where their tins were hidden and fetch them to the cave. Perhaps between them they could carry one sack.

'We'd better go now,' said Jack. 'We'll have to keep a sharp lookout for those men, because they were going to have a jolly good look round, and we don't want them to spot us. Now, you're sure you girls will be all right?'

'Quite,' said Dinah lazily. She felt glad she was not going to go all the way back to the bush and then drag a heavy sack to the cave. She lay back on the moss. It was so very very soft, and springy too.

Jack slung his field glasses round him. They might be useful in trying to spot any men from far off. He and Philip slid through the green fronds of fern. Jack called back to the girls, raising his voice high.

'If you *should* happen to spot anyone near here, remember to untie the string that ties back these ferns *at once*, see?' he said. 'Then they will swing back and the cave will be completely hidden. Lucy-Ann, see that Kiki doesn't follow us.'

Lucy-Ann had Kiki on her shoulder, where Jack had just put her. She put her hand round the bird's ankles and held her. Kiki knew then that she was not supposed to go with Jack and Philip and she gave a dismal squawk.

'What a pity, what a pity!' she said gloomily, and raised up her crest fiercely. But Lucy-Ann would not let her go. She held her until Jack and Philip were out of sight. Then she lowered her hand and Kiki flew off her shoulder and out of the cave. She perched on a rock looking for Jack.

'Down the well,' she said grumpily. 'Blackbirds down the well.'

'No, blackbirds in a pie,' said Lucy. 'What a bird you are for getting things mixed up, Kiki!'

'Poor Kiki!' said Kiki, and cracked her beak loudly. 'Poor Kiki!'

She flew back into the cave. Dinah was fast asleep, stretched out on the green moss, her mouth open. Kiki flew over and put her head on one side, looking at Dinah's open mouth. Then she plucked up a bit of moss with her curved beak.

'Kiki! Don't you dare to put that into Dinah's mouth!' cried Lucy-Ann, knowing Kiki's mischievous ways. 'You're a bad bird!'

'Wipe your feet,' said Kiki crossly, and flew to the

back of the cave. Lucy-Ann turned over on her tummy and watched her. She didn't trust Kiki in this mood.

The sun poured into the cave. It felt breathless in there. Lucy-Ann thought it would be a good idea to untie the fronds and let them swing together, to keep out the sun. So she pulled the bit of string that Jack had shown her and at once the ferny curtain descended, and the cave was lost in a dim green twilight, rather exciting to be in.

Dinah didn't wake. Lucy-Ann lay on her tummy again, thinking of all that had happened. The noise of the waterfall came in, rather muffled now, for the curtain of fronds was very thick.

'Kiki,' said Lucy-Ann. 'Kiki, where are you?'

There was no answer from Kiki. Lucy-Ann tried to make out where the parrot was. She must be sulking because Philip and Jack hadn't taken her with them. Silly old Kiki!

'Kiki! Come over here!' said Lucy-Ann. 'Come and talk to me. I'll teach you "Three little kittens have lost their mittens".'

Still there was no answer from Kiki, not even a squawk. Lucy-Ann wondered why. Even if Kiki sulked she would usually talk back if anyone spoke to her.

She peered towards the back of the cave. No Kiki there. She looked at the ledge on which their goods were neatly arranged. No Kiki there.

Well, where was she then? She hadn't flown out

between the fern fronds, that was certain. She must be *somewhere* in the cave!

On the rocky ledge was a torch. Lucy-Ann felt for it and took it into her hand. She switched it on and flashed it round the cave. Kiki was nowhere to be seen. She was not even perched up anywhere in the low roof of the cave. How very mysterious!

Lucy-Ann now felt quite alarmed. She awoke Dinah, who sat up, rubbing her eyes, cross to be awakened.

'What's the matter?' she said. 'I was having such a lovely snooze.'

'I can't find Kiki,' said Lucy-Ann. 'I've looked everywhere.'

'Don't be silly. She's gone out of the cave after Jack, I expect,' said Dinah, even crosser. She lay down again and yawned. Lucy-Ann shook her.

'You're not to go to sleep again, Dinah. I tell you, Kiki was here a little while ago – at the back of the cave – and now she's gone. Absolutely vanished.'

'Well, let her – she'll come back all right,' said Dinah. 'Leave me alone, Lucy-Ann.'

She shut her eyes. Lucy-Ann didn't like to say any more. Dinah could be so fierce when she was cross. The little girl sighed and wished the boys were back. What *had* happened to Kiki?

She got up and walked across the moss to the back of the cave. The rock was folded in on itself there, and there was a space behind one of the folds. Lucy-Ann looked cautiously into the dark space, expecting to see Kiki hiding there, ready to cry 'Boo' at her, as she sometimes most annoyingly did.

But Kiki wasn't there. Lucy-Ann flashed her torch up and down the little hidden corner, and suddenly her torch came to a stop, focused on one place.

'Why – there's a hole there!' said Lucy-Ann in surprise. 'That's where Kiki must have gone!'

She clambered up to the hole, which was about shoulder-high. It was just big enough for her to squeeze through. She expected to drop down into another cave the other side, but she didn't. The hole went upwards slightly, a round, narrow tunnel. Lucy-Ann felt sure Kiki must have disappeared into this cold, dark little tunnel.

'Kiki!' she yelled, and flashed her torch in front of her. 'Where are you, idiot? Come back!'

No sound from Kiki. Lucy-Ann squeezed herself right into the round tunnel, wondering how long it was. It was almost as round as a pipe. Maybe water had forced its way through at one time, but now it was quite dry. Lucy-Ann could not hear any sound of the waterfall once she was in the tunnel, though she listened hard. It was very quiet there.

'KIKI!' she yelled. 'KIKI!'

Dinah heard the yell in her dreams and awoke with a jump. She sat up crossly again. But this time Lucy-Ann was not in the cave with her. Now it was Dinah's turn to feel scared. She remembered that Lucy-Ann said that

Kiki had suddenly disappeared. Now it seemed as if Lucy-Ann had too. The fronds of fern were hanging over the entrance, Lucy-Ann would not have pushed out through them without telling Dinah she was going out.

Dinah examined the cave well. No Lucy-Ann. Oh, goodness, now what had happened to her and Kiki?

She heard another yell, sounding rather muffled and distant. She went to the back of the cave and discovered the hidden space. She fetched another torch from the ledge and shone it up and down. She stared in amazement when she saw two shoes sticking out of a round hole about as high as her shoulder.

She tugged at Lucy-Ann's ankles and yelled at her. 'Lucy-Ann! What *do* you think you're doing? What's up that hole?'

Lucy-Ann yelled back. 'I don't know, Dinah. I found it by accident. I think Kiki must have gone up it. Shall I go up and see if I can find her? You come too.'

'All right,' called Dinah. 'Go on up.'

Lucy-Ann wriggled further up the narrow pipe-like tunnel. It suddenly widened out, and by the light of her torch she saw below her another cave – but a vast one this time.

She managed to get out of the hole, and had a look round at the cave. It was more like an underground hall. Its roof was very high indeed. From somewhere in its dim vastness came a mournful voice.

'What a pity, what a pity!'

'Kiki! So you are here!' cried Lucy-Ann, and then listened in astonishment to the echo that sounded immediately. 'Here, here, here, are here, and here!' cried the echoes, repeating themselves in a weird and strange manner.

'Hurry up, Dinah!' called Lucy-Ann, not liking the echoes at all.

'Up, Dinah, Dinah, Dinah!' called the echoes at once. Kiki flew over to Lucy-Ann, frightened. So many voices! Whatever could they all be?

'Poor Kiki!' said the parrot, in a fright. 'Poor Kiki!'

'Kiki, Kiki, Kiki!' called the echoes. The parrot shivered and gazed all round, trying to see who called her. She suddenly gave a loud and defiant squawk.

At once a score of squawks sounded all round, as if the cave was filled with hundred of parrots. Kiki was simply astounded. *Could* there be so many birds there that she couldn't see?

Dinah crawled out of the hole and stood by Lucy-Ann. 'What an enormous place!' she said.

'Place!' shouted the echoes.

'Everything we say is repeated,' said Lucy-Ann. 'It's weird.'

'Weird, it's weird,' said the echoes.

'Well, let's whisper then,' said Dinah, whispering herself. The cave was at once filled with mysterious whispers, which scared the girls even more than the repeated shouts they had heard. They clutched one another. Then Dinah recovered herself.

'It's only the echoes,' she said. 'You often get them in enormous caves like this. I wonder if anyone has ever been here before.'

'Never, I should think,' said Lucy-Ann, flashing her torch all round. 'Fancy! We may be treading in a place that no one else has ever trodden in before!'

'Let's explore the cave a bit,' said Dinah. 'Not that there seems much to see, but we might as well do something whilst we're waiting for the boys.'

So they walked slowly round the great dark cave, their footsteps repeated a hundred times by the echoes. Once, when Dinah sneezed, the girls were really frightened by the enormous explosive noises that came from all round them. The echoes certainly enjoyed themselves then.

'Oh, don't sneeze again, Dinah,' begged Lucy-Ann. 'It's really awful to hear the echoes sneezing. Worse than hearing them squawk like Kiki.'

They had gone almost all the way round the cave when they came to a passage leading out of it – a high, narrow passage, between two walls of rocks.

'Look at that!' said Dinah, surprised. 'A passage! Do you suppose it leads anywhere?'

'It might,' said Lucy-Ann, and her eyes gleamed. 'Don't forget, Dinah, that those men are after treasure. We don't know what kind – but it's just possible it might be hidden somewhere in these mountains.'

'Let's follow the passage then,' said Dinah. 'Kiki! Come along. We don't want to leave you behind.'

Kiki flew to her shoulder. In silence the two girls entered the narrow, rocky passage, their torches gleaming in front of them. What were they going to find?

12

Behind the waterfall

The passage was a very winding one. It led a little downwards, and the floor was very uneven to the feet. The girls tripped and stumbled very often. Once the roof came down so low that they had to crawl under it. But it grew high again almost at once.

After a while they heard a noise. They couldn't imagine what it was. It was a deep and continous roar that never stopped even for a second.

'What's that?' said Dinah. 'Are we getting into the heart of the mountain, do you think, Lucy-Ann? That's not the roar of a mighty fire, is it? What can it be? What is there that could make that noise in the middle of a mountain?'

'I don't know,' said Lucy-Ann, and immediately wanted to go back. A fire in the heart of a mountain, a fire that roared like that? She didn't in the least want to see it. She felt hot and breathless at the thought.

But Dinah wasn't going back now that they had come so far.

'What, go back before we've found out where this passage goes to?' she said. 'Of course not! The boys would laugh like anything when we told them. We don't often get the chance of discovering something before they do. Why, we might even happen on the treasure, whatever it is, Lucy-Ann.'

Lucy-Ann felt that she didn't care at all about the treasure. All she wanted was to get back to the safety of the cave with the green fern curtains.

'Well, you go back then,' said Dinah unkindly. 'I'm going on!'

It was more frightening to think of going back to the cave of echoes by herself than to go on with Dinah. So poor Lucy-Ann chose unwillingly to go on. With that peculiar, muffled roar in her ears she pressed on down the winding passage, keeping close to Dinah. The roar became louder.

And then the girls knew what it was. It was the waterfall, of course! How stupid of them not to think of that! But it sounded so different there in the mountain.

'We're *not* going into the heart of the mountain after all,' said Dinah. 'We're coming out somewhere near the waterfall. I wonder where.'

They got a tremendous surprise when they did see daylight. The passage suddenly took one last turn and took them into subdued daylight, that flickered and shone round them in a curious way. A draught of cold air met them, and something wetted their hair.

'Lucy-Ann! We've come out on to a flat ledge just *behind* the waterfall!' cried Dinah in astonishment. 'Look, there's the great mass of falling water just in front of us! – oh, the colours in it! Can you hear me? The water is making such a noise.'

Overwhelmed by surprise and by the noise, Lucy-Ann stood and stared. The water made a great rushing curtain between them and the open air. It poured down, shining and exultant, never stopping. The power behind it awed the two girls. They felt very small and feeble when they watched the great volume of water pouring down a few feet in front of them.

It was amazing to be able to stand on a ledge just behind the waterfall and yet not to be affected by it in any way except to feel the fine spray misting the air. The ledge was very wide, and ran the whole width of the fall. There was a rock about a foot high at one end of the ledge, and the girls sat down on it to watch the amazing sight in front of them.

'What will the boys say?' wondered Dinah. 'Let's stay here till we see them coming back. If we sit on this rock, just at the edge of the waterfall, we can wave to them. They will be so astonished to see us here. There's no way of getting to the ledge from above or below, only from behind, from the passage we found.'

'Yes. We'll surprise the boys,' said Lucy-Ann, no

longer frightened. 'Look, we can see our cave up there! – at least, we can see the giant fern whose fronds are hiding it. We shall easily be able to see the boys when they come back.'

Kiki was very quiet indeed. She had been surprised to come out behind the great wall of water. She sat on a ledge and watched it, blinking every now and again.

'I hope she won't be silly enough to try and fly through the waterfall,' said Lucy-Ann anxiously. 'She would be taken down with it and dashed to pieces. I know she would.'

'She won't do anything silly,' said Dinah. 'She's wise enough to know what would happen if she tried something like that. She may fly out round the edge of the waterfall, though. Still, there shouldn't be much danger for her in that.'

The girls sat there for a long time, feeling that they would never get tired of watching the turbulence of the waterfall. After a long time Lucy-Ann gave a cry and caught Dinah's arm.

'Look – is that the boys coming? Yes, it is. They've got a sack between them. Good! Now we shall have plenty of food.'

They watched the two boys labouring up the rocks that led to the cave. It was no good waving to them yet. Then suddenly Dinah stiffened with horror.

'What's the matter?' said Lucy-Ann in alarm, seeing Dinah's face.

'Look – someone is following the boys!' said Dinah. 'See – it's one of the men! And there's the other one too! Oh, my goodness, I don't believe either Philip or Jack knows it! They'll watch where they go and our hiding place will be found! JACK! PHILIP! OH, JACK, LOOK OUT!'

She went to the very edge of the waterfall, and, holding on to a fern growing there, she leaned out beyond it, yelling and waving, quite forgetting that the men could see and hear her as well as the boys.

But alas, Jack and Philip, engrossed in the task of getting the heavy sack up the rocks, neither saw nor heard Dinah – but the men suddenly caught sight of her and stared in the utmost astonishment. They could not make out if she was girl, boy, or woman, for the edges of the waterfall continually moved and shifted. All they could make out was that there was definitely someone dancing about and waving behind the great fall.

'Look!' said one man to the other. 'Just look at that! See – behind the water! That's where they're hiding. My word, what a place! How do they get there?'

The men stared open-mouthed at the waterfall, their eyes searching for a way up to it that would lead to the ledge where the excited figure stood waving.

Meantime, Jack and Philip, quite unaware of the following men, or of Dinah either, had reached the curtain of fern. Philip pushed the ferns aside, and Jack hauled the sack up through them, panting painfully, for it was heavy.

At last the sack lay on the floor of moss. The boys flung themselves down, their hearts thumping with the labour of climbing up steeply to the cave, dragging such a heavy sack. At first they did not even notice that the girls were not there.

Not far off, some way below, stood the two men, completely bewildered. In watching Dinah behind the waterfall, they had just missed seeing Jack and Philip creep through the ferns into their cave. So when they turned from gazing at the waterfall, they found that the boys they had so warily followed had utterly disappeared.

'Where have they gone?' demanded Juan. 'They were on that rock there when we saw them last.'

'Yes. Then I caught sight of that person waving down there, and took my eyes off them for a minute – and now they've gone,' growled Pepi. 'Well, there's no doubt where they've gone. They've taken some path that leads to that waterfall. They hide behind it – and a clever place it is too. Who would think of anyone hiding just behind a great curtain of water like that? Well, we know where to find them. We'll make our way to the water and climb up to that ledge. We'll soon hunt the rats out.'

They began to climb down, hoping to find a way that would lead them to the ledge behind the waterfall. It was difficult and dangerous going, on the slippery rocks.

In the cave the boys soon recovered. They sat up, and looked around for the girls.

'Hallo – where are Lucy-Ann and Dinah?' said Jack in

astonishment. 'They promised to stay here till we got back. Surely to goodness they haven't gone wandering about anywhere? They'll get lost, sure as anything!'

They were not in the cave. That was absolutely certain. The boys did not see the hole in the fold of rock at the back. They were extremely puzzled. Jack parted the ferns and looked out.

To his enormous astonishment he at once saw the two men clambering about on rocks near the waterfall. His eyes nearly dropped out of his head.

'Look there!' he said to Philip, closing the fronds a little, fearful of being seen. 'Those two men! Golly, they might have seen us getting in here! How did they get here? We saw them safely by the plane, on our way to the bush!'

Dinah had now disappeared from behind the waterfall. She could not make up her mind whether or not the men had seen the boys climbing in through the fern to their cave. In any case, she thought she ought to warn them of the men's appearance. She felt sure that neither Jack nor Philip knew they were there.

'Come on, Lucy-Ann,' she said urgently. 'We must get back to the boys. Oh, goodness, look at those men! I believe they are going to try and get over here now. They must have spotted me waving. Do come quickly, Lucy-Ann.'

Shivering with excitement, Lucy-Ann followed Dinah along the dark, winding passage that led back to the cave of echoes. Dinah went as quickly as she could, flashing her torch in front of her. Both girls forgot all about Kiki. The parrot was left sitting alone behind the waterfall, spray misting her feathers, watched the clambering men with interested eyes. She had not heard the girls going off.

Dinah and Lucy-Ann came out into the cave of echoes at last. Dinah stopped and considered. 'Now, where exactly was that hole we came through?' she said.

'Came through, through, through,' called the echoes mockingly.

'Oh be *quiet*!' cried Dinah to the echoes.

'QUIET, QUIET, QUIET!' yelled back the irritating voices. Dinah flashed her torch here and there, and by a very lucky chance she found the hole. In a trice she was in it, crawling along, with Lucy-Ann close behind her. Lucy-Ann had an awful feeling that somebody was going to clutch her feet from behind and she almost bumped into Dinah's shoes in her efforts to scramble down the hole as quickly as possible.

Jack and Philip were peeping through the ferns watching the men, when the girls dropped out of the hole at the back of the cave, came round the fold of rock and flung themselves on the boys. They almost jumped out of their skin.

Philip hit out, thinking that enemies were upon them. Dinah got a stinging blow on the ear, and yelled.

She immediately hit out at Philip and the two rolled on the floor.

'Don't, oh, don't!' wailed Lucy-Ann, almost in tears. 'Philip, Jack, it's us! It's us!'

Philip shook off Dinah and sat up. Jack stared in amazement. 'But where did you come from?' he demanded. 'Golly, you gave us an awful scare, I can tell you, jumping out like that! Where have you been?'

'There's a hole back there we went into,' explained Dinah, giving Philip an angry look. 'I say, do you two boys know that those men were following you? They were not very far behind you. We were scared stiff they would see you climbing in here.'

'Were they *following* us!' said Jack. 'Golly, I didn't know that. Peep out between these fronds, you girls, and see them hunting for us down there.'

13

Safe in the Cave

They all peeped out between the fern fronds, Lucy-Ann holding her breath. Yes, there were the two men, clambering about dangerously near the waterfall.

'But what are they doing down *there*?' said Jack in wonder. 'Why look for us there? They must have know we didn't go that way, if they were following us.'

'Well, they must have seen me waving to you from behind the waterfall,' said Dinah. 'They must think that's where our hiding place is.'

'Waving to us from behind the waterfall?' said Philip in the utmost amazement. 'What are you talking about, Dinah? You must be bats.'

'Well, I'm not,' said Dinah. 'That's where Lucy-Ann and I were when you came up the slope there to climb into the cave. We were standing behind the waterfall, and I tried my hardest to attract your attention and tell you that those two men were following you.'

'But – how in the world did you get *behind* the

waterfall?' asked Jack. 'It was an idiotic thing to do. Fancy climbing up those slippery rocks, and getting behind the water! You might have been . . .'

'We didn't go that way, silly,' said Dinah. 'We went another way.' And she told Jack and Philip all about the hole at the back of the cave that led down into the cave of echoes, and the passage that came out behind the roaring waterfall. The boys listened in the greatest amazement.

'Gosh! How extraordinary!' said Jack. 'Well, I suppose the men just caught sight of you down there, Dinah, and took their eyes off me and Philip for a minute, and lost us. We must have climbed into this cave through the fern just as they were watching you. What a good thing!'

'That's why they're messing about down there on those wet rocks,' said Philip, grinning. 'They think that that is our hiding place, behind the fall, and they want to get there and find us. They don't guess that isn't the right way. I can't for the life of me see how they can possibly get behind the water from any of those rocks in front. If they're not jolly careful, they'll get swept off by the water – and down they'll go like lightning.'

Lucy-Ann shuddered. 'I don't want to see them do that,' she said, and wouldn't peep out of the ferns any more.

But Dinah and the boys watched in glee. They felt safe up there in their fern-hidden cave, and it was fun to watch the two men slipping about on the rocks near the water, getting angrier and angrier.

Kiki was still behind the waterfall, watching them with interest. Suddenly she gave one of her dreadful cackles of laughter, and the men heard it even through the roar of the water. They looked at one another, startled.

'Hear that?' said Juan. 'Somebody yelling their heads off, laughing at us. Wait till I get them, that's all. They must be just behind the sheet of water. How *do* they get there?'

It was impossible to get behind the waterfall from above or below. Quite impossible. The men realised this after they had fallen many times, and once almost slipped off a wet rock into the cascading water itself. They sat down on a ledge a good way from the water and mopped their heads. They were hot and angry, and their clothes were soaked.

They were puzzled too. Where had those boys come from? Was there a whole camp of people somewhere? Were they hiding in the mountains? No, that could not be so, for they would have seen them roving the countryside in search of food. There could only be a few people. They must have sent out the boys to seek for food.

The children watched in delight. There was something very enjoyable in seeing their enemies at a loss, in being able to see their every action and yet not be seen

111

themselves. Even Lucy-Ann had another peep now that she knew they were no longer slipping about the waterfall.

'We'd better go,' said Juan. 'If that's their hiding place they can keep it. We'd better get somebody else here to help us. We could put him to guard this place. If he sat here, he could see if anyone came up to get behind the water. Come on, I'm fed up with this.'

They stood up. Jack watched them through the fern fronds. Were they going back to their hut, or to the plane, perhaps? Then, seeing that they were going to pass rather near to the cave, the boy hastily closed the fronds and pushed the others back.

'Keep quiet,' he said. 'They may come fairly near.'

They came extremely near. They took a way that led them right past the cave itself. The children sat as still as stone, hearing the men scrambling along outside. Suddenly the fern swayed and shook, and Lucy-Ann's hand flew up to her mouth to stifle a scream.

'They're coming in, they've found us,' she thought, and her heart almost stopped beating. The fern rustled again, and then there was quiet. The footsteps passed, and the children heard the voices of the two men saying something they could not catch.

'Have they gone?' wondered Dinah, and looking at Jack, she raised her eyebrows. He nodded. Yes – they were gone – but what a terrible fright everyone had had when they grasped hold of the fern to help them along!

Little did Juan and Pepi dream that four silent children sat within two feet of them then.

Jack parted the fern again. There was no sign of the men. He felt sure they must have gone back, but he did not dare to go out and spy. 'Better lie low for a bit,' he said. 'We'll have a meal. I'll creep out and spy around later on. Where's Kiki?'

Nobody knew. Then Dinah remembered she had been with them behind the waterfall. They had gone back without her in their anxiety to warn the boys about the two men. She must still be there.

'Blow! We'd better go and fetch her,' said Jack. 'I don't really feel like moving just now, either – I'm really tired with dragging that heavy sack along so far.'

A voice spoke outside the cave . . . a gloomy, dismal, reproachful voice.

'Poor Kiki! All alone! What a pity, what a Kiki, poor pity!'

The children laughed, and Jack parted the fronds cautiously, in case by any chance the men were still anywhere about. Kiki clambered through, looking very sorry for herself. She flew to Jack's shoulder and nibbled his ear gently.

'All aboard!' she said more cheerfully, and cracked her beak. Dinah ruffled up the feathers on her head.

'Kiki must have flown out from behind the waterfall and come straight here,' she said. 'Clever Kiki! clever old bird!'

'God save the Queen,' said Kiki. 'Wipe your feet!'

Jack's tin-opener came out again, and a choice of tins and jars was made. There was a small tin of biscuits still to be finished, and the children chose some pressed meat to go with them, and a large tin of juicy apricots. Jack opened the fronds just a little to let in enough daylight to see by. Once again they thoroughly enjoyed their meal, and Kiki got into trouble for taking more than her fair share of apricots.

The children waited some time before they dared to creep out of the cave. When the sun was well down, Jack clambered out between the fronds, and had a good look round. There was no sign of the men at all. Jack found a high place from which, if he sat there, he could see for a good way in any direction.

'We'll take it in turns to keep watch,' he said. 'You can come in half an hour, Philip.'

They had a fine time clambering all about. They found some wild raspberries, and ate great quantities of them. They were delicious. Kiki ate them too, murmuring 'Mmmmmmmmm' all the time.

Each of them took turn at keeping watch, but there was nothing to see. The sun went down behind behind the mountains, and twilight came. They all went back to the cave.

'It will be lovely to sleep here tonight,' said Lucy-Ann, pleased. 'This moss is so nice and soft. Like velvet.'

She stroked it. It *felt* like velvet too. She helped Dinah

to put down macks and a rug to lie on, and made pillows of pullovers and jerseys.

'A drink of apricot juice and a few biscuits for everyone,' said Dinah, as they all sat down on the 'bed.' She handed out the biscuits. Jack parted the fern fronds and tied them firmly back.

'Must have a little air in the cave,' he said. 'It will get jolly stuffy with four of us here.'

'Five,' said Dinah. 'Don't forget Kiki.'

'Six,' said Philip, producing the lizard. 'Don't forget Dizzy Lizzie.'

'Oh, I really hoped you'd lost her,' said Dinah crossly. 'I haven't seen her all day.'

They finished their biscuits and lay down. It was quite dark now outside. Their 'bed' felt warm and soft. They all snuggled down, making nice cosy places for themselves.

'I should really enjoy this, if only I knew that Mother wasn't worrying about us,' said Philip, pulling the rug over him. 'I haven't any idea at all where we are, but it's a very beautiful place. Doesn't that waterfall sound lovely, singing in the night?'

'It's singing jolly loudly,' said Jack, yawning. 'But I don't think it will keep *me* awake. Oh, Kiki, do move off my middle. I can't imagine why you will keep perching there at night. Go on one of my feet.'

'Wipe your feet,' ordered Kiki, and flew to Jack's right foot. She put her head under her wing.

'Tomorrow Philip and I must go to that cave of echoes you told us about and stand behind the waterfall,' said Jack. 'Fancy you girls having a little adventure like that all on your own!'

'*Little* adventure!' said Lucy-Ann. 'Why, it was a jolly big one – especially when we suddenly saw that we were just behind the waterfall!'

Dinah was very much afraid that Lizzie would run over her during the night, and lay awake some time expecting the feel of her tiny feet. But Lizzie was curled up in Philip's armpit, tickling him dreadfully when she moved.

Lucy-Ann was asleep almost at once, and soon the others were too. The waterfall roared all through the night without ceasing. The wind sprang up and moved the big fronds of the fern. A fox or some other creature came sniffing up to the cave entrance, was alarmed at the smell of humans there and fled away silently.

Nobody stirred, except Philip when the lizard woke up, felt cramped, and made her way to another nice warm spot, this time behind his ear. He awoke for a second, felt Lizzie moving, and then shut his eyes immediately again, pleased with the feel of the tiny feet.

Towards morning a throbbing sound awoke all four children. It penetrated into the cave, sounding even louder than the waterfall. Jack sat up at once, surprised. What could that be?

The noise grew louder and louder; it seemed as if it

was coming right down on their heads. Whatever *could* it be?

Rr-rr-rr-rr-rr-rrRRRRRRRRRRRRRRRRR!

'It's a plane!' cried Jack. 'A plane! Come to rescue us. Out of the cave, quick!'

They all tumbled out of the cave and looked for the plane. One was climbing into the air, a large shape against the sky. It had evidently come very near the side of the mountain, and had awakened them by its noise.

'A plane to rescue us?' said Philip scornfully. 'Not likely! That's the plane we came here in – the men's plane, idiot!'

14

The poor prisoner

Sure enough, it was the men's plane. The children all recognised it quite well as they watched it vanishing into the distance. It flew towards the west.

'Wonder if it's going back to Bill's aerodrome?' said Jack. 'Wonder if Bill knows what those men are up to?'

'We don't know very much ourselves, except that they are after some sort of treasure,' said Philip. 'But, honestly, what treasure they think they can find here in this place beats me.'

'Beats me too,' said Jack. 'Well – there they go! Do you suppose they'll come back?'

'Sure to,' said Philip. 'They won't give up as easily as that. Maybe they've gone to report that there are other people here now – for all they know, after the treasure too! And they might bring back more men to smell us out.'

'Oh,' said Lucy-Ann in alarm. 'I don't want to be smelt out.'

'Do you think *both* men have gone?' asked Philip.

'I should think so,' said Jack. 'But we can go and have a jolly good look round and see. If one man is left, he'll be somewhere near that shed of theirs. He won't know how many of us there are here – he may think there are men with us, you know, and not dare to move about too much by himself.'

But when the children left the cave later in the morning and went to 'have a squint,' as Jack said, they could find no sign of either Juan or Pepi. There was no fire. It had been stamped out. And this time the shed was well and truly locked, and the key taken. No amount of shaking or kicking would open the door.

'Well, if we'd known the men were going to fly off, we might have asked them for a lift,' said Jack with a grin. 'I wonder when they'll come back – if they do come back, that is.'

'Not till it's daylight tomorrow, I should think,' said Philip. 'I expect they'll take off at night again. Let's go and have another squint at those crates.'

But there was really nothing to see. They were empty as before, and the tarpaulin was over them. The children played about for some hours, and had a meal under a tree. They went to get a tin or two from the rest of the store still hidden in the bush. Jack opened them.

After the meal Philip suggested that they should go back to the waterfall and the girls should take them to the cave of echoes, and down the passage that led behind the water. So off they went, first hiding all trace of having been near the men's shed.

But when they got back to their cave, Jack gave a most annoyed exclamation and began to feel in all his pockets.

'What's the matter?' said Lucy-Ann.

'Well, do you know what I've done? I've gone and left the tin-opener behind,' said Jack. 'Think of that! What an idiotic thing to do! I thought we might want another tin opened, so I put it down at the roots of that tree we had our picnic under – and I must have left it there. I haven't got it, anyway.'

'Oh, *Jack*! But we can't have a meal without opening a tin,' said Philip, seeing awful visions of a hungry night. 'Gosh – you *are* an ass!'

'Yes, I know,' said Jack gloomily. 'Well, there's only one thing to be done. I must go back and get it. You explore the cave of echoes with the girls, Philip, and I'll take Kiki and go back for the opener. Serves me right.'

'I'll come with you, Jack,' said Lucy-Ann, sorry for her brother.

'No, you've had a jolly long walk already,' said Jack. 'You go with the others. Anyway, I'll be quicker by myself. I'll just have a sitdown before I start back. I can always explore the cave another time.'

He sat down on the moss. The others sat with him, sorry for him, knowing how annoyed he must feel with himself. But it would be still more annoying to have to go without meals. The opener must certainly be fetched.

After about half an hour Jack felt able to start back again. He said a cheery goodbye to the others, and left, scrambling quickly down the rocks. They knew he would not lose his way. They all felt they knew it quite well by this time.

Jack had Kiki on his shoulder, and they talked together all the way. Kiki was simply delighted to have Jack all to herself. He was nearly always with the others. They talked complete nonsense and both of them thoroughly enjoyed it.

Jack arrived at last at the tree under which they had had their lunch. He looked for the opener, half fearful in case it had been removed by somebody. But it was still there, lying where he had left it. He picked it up and put it into his pocket.

'Three cheers,' he said.

'Three blind mice,' said Kiki. 'Handy spandy, humpy dumpy.'

'I agree with you,' said Jack. 'Well, we'll get back, I think. Twilight will soon be coming and I don't fancy going back in the dark. Off we go, Kiki, up the hill.'

'Jack and Jill,' agreed Kiki.

'Jack and Kiki, you mean,' grinned Jack, turning to go. Then he stood still suddenly and listened. Away in the distance he could hear a sound he knew – a familiar, throbbing sound. Rr-rr-rr-rr-rr!

'Gosh, Kiki! – are those fellows coming back so soon?' said Jack, staring into the western sky, which was still faintly gold. 'Yes – that's a plane all right. But is it theirs?'

The plane came nearer, growing larger and larger. An idea came into Jack's mind. He ran to where the men's shed was, and climbed quickly up into a tree not far from where they had their camp-fire. He spoke sternly to Kiki.

'Now, quiet, Kiki. Not a word. Do you understand? Shhhhhhh!'

'What a pity, what a pity!' said Kiki in a curious hoarse whisper, and then was silent, pressing against Jack's neck as she sat on his shoulder.

The plane roared nearer. It circled lower and lower. It dropped to the long smooth strip that made such an excellent runway. It bounced along on its high wheels and then came to a stop. Jack could not see the plane from where he was.

But he was counting on the men coming to the shed or to their fire, and he was right. They soon arrived, and Jack peered out through the leaves, nearly overbalancing in his efforts to see properly, for twilight was almost there.

This time there were four men. Jack looked very hard. He could see that one man was evidently a prisoner. He had his hands tied behind him. How strange!

He shambled along, his head bent, going from side to side a little as if he was dizzy. Now and again one of the others would give him a shove to keep him straight. They came straight to the campfire.

Juan set to work to light it. Pepi went off to the shed to get some tins. He took a key from his pocket and unlocked the door. He came out carrying tins of soup and meat.

The prisoner sat down on the grass, his head bent. It was obvious that he was not feeling well – or was he merely afraid? Jack couldn't tell. The fourth man, who was a kind of guard for the prisoner, as far as Jack could make out, sat by the fire saying nothing, watching Juan and Pepi.

At first they talked in low voices and Jack could not hear their words. They drank hot soup, and then carved up a tongue from a glass jar. They ate bread with it which they had brought from the plane. The prisoner looked up and saw them eating, but the three men did not offer him anything. He said something in a low voice. Juan laughed.

He spoke to the guard. 'Tell him he won't get anything to eat or drink till he tells us what we want to know,' he said.

The guard repeated this in some language that Jack could not make out. The prisoner said something and the guard struck him on the cheek. Jack watched in horror. Fancy hitting a man when his hands were tied! What cowards!

The man tried to dodge. He bent his head again and sat dismally there.

'He says you've got the map, what else do you want?' said the guard.

'We can't read the map,' said Juan. 'It's all messed up. If he can't explain it to us, he'll have to show us the way tomorrow.'

The guard translated this to the prisoner. He shook his head. 'He says he is too weak to walk so far,' said the guard.

'We'll drag him all right,' said Pepi, and took another piece of tongue, making himself a thick sandwich. 'Tell him he's to take us tomorrow. If he won't, he gets nothing to eat or drink. He'll soon come round when he's half starved.'

They finished their meal. Then Juan yawned. 'Me for bed,' he said. 'There's a chair for you, Luis, in the hut. The floor's good enough for the prisoner.'

The man begged to have his hands untied, but they would not allow him to. Jack felt very sorry for him. They stamped out the fire and went to the hut. Jack imagined Pepi and Juan on the mattress, and Luis in the only comfortable chair. The poor prisoner would have to lie on the cold, hard floor, with his hands still tied behind him.

Jack waited till he thought the coast was clear, then he slipped quietly down the tree. Kiki had been as good as gold all the time. Not even a whisper had come from her beak. Jack tiptoed to the hut. He peeped cautiously in at the window. A candle burned in the hut, and by its flickering light he could make out the four men. The prisoner was trying to make himself comfortable on the floor.

It was almost dark. Jack hoped he would be able to get back to the cave all right. He slipped his hand into his pocket and was relieved to find a small torch there. That was good!

He was very clever in the dark, for he had eyes like a cat. Once or twice he stopped, unable to think which way to go – but Kiki always knew. She simply flew a little way in front and called to him, or whistled.

'Good old Kiki!' said Jack. 'I couldn't find my way without you, that's certain.'

The others were very worried about him. When darkness fell and still no Jack had arrived, Lucy-Ann wanted to go and look for him.

'I'm sure he's lost, I'm certain of it,' she said, almost in tears.

'Yes, and *we'd* all get lost too, if we went out on the mountainside in this darkness,' said Philip. 'I expect he hunted about for that opener, saw that twilight was coming and decided not to risk coming back in the dark. He'll be back tomorrow morning early, for certain.'

It was too dark to do anything. Dinah had made the 'bed' and they lay down on it, Lucy-Ann very worried. She was sure something had happened to Jack.

Then there came a scrambling noise up near the cave, and the fern was parted and pushed aside. All the children sat up, their hearts beating. Was it Jack – or had their hiding place been discovered?

'Hallo, there!' came Jack's familiar voice. 'Where's everybody?'

He switched on his torch and saw three delighted faces. Lucy-Ann almost fell on him.

'Jack! We thought you were lost. What *have* you been doing? And we're so hungry too. Have you brought the tin-opener?'

'Yes, I've brought that – and plenty of news as well!' said Jack. 'What about a meal whilst I tell you all about it?'

15

A disappointment for the men

Tins were opened once more, and Kiki gave a delighted chortle at the sight of her favourite pineapple. Lucy-Ann pressed close to Jack.

'What happened to you? I can't wait to hear. Tell me quickly.'

'Let me have a bite first,' said Jack irritatingly, knowing quite well that all the others were longing to hear his news. But as he was longing just as much to tell it as they were to hear it, he soon began his story.

'So the plane's back!' exclaimed Philip, as Jack began to tell everything. 'Both men back too?'

Jack told of the four men. Lucy-Ann was distressed to hear about the poor prisoner.

'I'm beginning to see daylight,' said Philip at last. 'Somewhere in this valley is hidden treasure – maybe stuff belonging to the people whose houses have been burnt. Those two men heard about it, and somehow managed to get a map that showed them the hiding place. But they can't find it by that map, so they've got hold of somebody who knows the way.'

'That's it,' said Jack. 'He's foreign. Maybe he once belonged to this valley, and even hid the things himself. They've captured him and mean to make him show them the hiding-place. They're not giving him anything to eat or drink till he shows them what they want to know.'

'Brutes!' said Dinah, and the others agreed with her.

'Do you think he *will* show them?' asked Lucy-Ann.

'I hope he will for his own sake,' said Jack. 'And I'll tell you what I propose. I propose that somehow or other one or more of us follow them, and see where this hiding place is. The men can't possibly take everything away at once. We might be able to get help, and save the rest of the stuff being stolen by the men. It can't belong to them.'

'What do you think the stuff can be?' asked Lucy-Ann, visions of gold bars and beautiful jewels floating in her mind.

'Can't tell you,' said Jack. 'I think we're somewhere in the depths of Europe, where war has been, and as you know, plenty of treasure of all kinds was hidden in odd places by many, many people, good and bad. My guess is that it's something of that kind these men are after. They speak English, but they're not English. Perhaps from South America? Goodness knows.'

The others sat silent, thinking over what Jack had

said. They thought he was probably right. But Lucy-Ann didn't at all like the idea of following the men. Suppose they discovered that they were being followed, and captured them?

'It might be best if Philip and I did the stalking tomorrow,' said Jack. 'I don't think you girls should be mixed up in it.'

This made Dinah angry, though Lucy-Ann was secretly relieved.

'You're not going to keep all the excitement to yourselves,' said Dinah. 'I'm coming too.'

'No, you're not,' said Jack. He switched on his torch and shone it at Dinah's face. 'I thought you'd be glaring,' he said. 'Cheer up, Dinah. After all, you and Lucy-Ann had an adventure yesterday, when you found the cave of echoes and the passage that leads to the waterfall. Give us boys a chance.'

'Well, it's all very well,' grumbled Dinah, but she did not press the point any more, much to Lucy-Ann's relief.

'Where's Lizzie?' asked Dinah, not liking to settle down till she was quite sure of the lizard's whereabouts.

'Don't know,' said Philip annoyingly. 'She might be anywhere. Under your pillow, perhaps.'

'She's here,' said Jack. 'Kiki's one side of my neck and Lizzie's the other, keeping me nice and warm.'

'What a pity!' said Kiki, and cackled loudly.

'*Don't!*' said everybody at once. Nobody liked Kiki's awful cackle. She put her head under her wing, offended.

All the children lay down. They were sleepy. 'Our fourth night in this valley,' said Philip. 'The valley of adventure. I wonder what will happen next.'

Soon they were all asleep. Lizzie ran across Lucy-Ann and cuddled down by Dinah, who would certainly have objected strongly if she had known. But she didn't know. So she slept peacefully.

Everyone felt cheerful the next morning.

'Really,' said Dinah, reaching down some tins from the ledge, 'I'm beginning to feel I've made this cave my home half my life. It's extraordinary how soon we get used to anything new.'

'How are we going to find out when those men are starting, and what way they go?' said Philip.

'Well, if you remember, the two of them came in this direction, not the other, when they set out with the map before,' said Jack. 'I think if we go to that big black rock we always pass on the way here, we may spot them. Then we can follow easily enough.'

So when they had finished their meal they set off cautiously to the big black rock. They crouched behind it, and Jack kept peering out to see if there was anything to be seen.

After about an hour he gave a low exclamation. 'Hallo! Here they come – all four – prisoner still with his hands tied, stumbling along, poor thing.'

The four men passed some distance away. The children saw them well. They recognised the two men they knew, and Jack told them the fourth man was called Luis. The prisoner's name he didn't know. It was plain that the poor man was giddy for lack of food and drink.

'Now, you girls stay here, see?' said Jack. 'At any rate, till we are well out of sight. Then go back to the water-fall, and keep somewhere about there. Don't get lost! Take Kiki, Lucy-Ann. We don't want her with us.'

Lucy-Ann took Kiki and held her ankles. Kiki gave such an angry squawk that the children looked uneasily after the four men to see if by any chance they had heard. But they hadn't.

Jack and Philip made ready to set off. 'I've got my field glasses,' said Jack. 'I can keep the men well in sight, while following quite a long way behind, so that they won't spot us. Cheerio!'

The boys went off cautiously, keeping to every bit of cover they could. They could still see the men far away in the distance. 'Do we need to mark the way we're going?' asked Philip. 'Or shall we be able to find the way back, do you think?'

Better mark things where we can,' said Jack. 'You never know. Mark rocks with white chalk. Here's a bit. And trees we will notch.'

They went on, climbing upwards a good way behind the four men. Soon they came to a very steep place, difficult to keep their footing on, because the surface was so loose that they slid down continually.

'I hope they've undone that poor prisoner's hands,

panted Jack. 'I'd hate to do climbing like this and have my hands bound so that I couldn't save myself when I slipped.'

When they came to the end of the rough piece, the men were nowhere to be seen. 'Blow!' said Jack. 'That bit held us up too long. Now we've lost them!'

He put his field glasses to his eyes and swept the mountainside. Some way to the east and above them he suddenly saw four small figures. 'There they are!' he said. 'It's all right. I can see them. That way, Tufty.'

On they went again, going more quickly now because the way was easier. They picked wild raspberries as they went, and once stopped for a drink at a little clear spring of water that gushed from under a rock.

They did not lose sight of the men again except for a moment or two. The men did not turn round, or use field glasses at all. Plainly they did not expect anyone to follow them.

Now the boys came to a very desolate part of the mountainside. Big boulders had rolled down. Trees had been torn in half. Great ruts had been torn out of the earth and rock, and although the grass was growing everywhere to hide the scars, it was clear that some catastrophe had happened here.

'An avalanche, I should think,' said Jack. 'I guess a terrific fall of snow happened here – bringing down with it boulders and rocks of all sizes – knocking down trees and scoring those ruts. Last winter, I should think.'

'Where are the men?' said Philip. 'I can't see them now. They went round the ledge.'

'Yes. We'll have to be careful how we go round,' said Jack. 'We might easily be seen coming round there. There's not much cover in this devastated bit.'

So they went very cautiously round the ledge – and it was a good thing they did, for almost at once they heard voices and saw the four men.

Jack pressed Philip back. Just above the ledge was a bush. The boys climbed up to it, pressed against it, and parted the leaves so that they might see through. They found that they were looking down into a rocky gully.

Here, too, there had evidently been a great fall of rocks. In front of one heap stood the prisoner. His hands were now untied. He was pointing to the heap of rocks, and saying something in his rather dull, low voice. The guard translated, and Jack strained his ears to hear what he had to say.

'He says the entrance was here,' the guard said. The four men stared at the fall of rock.

'Exactly where?' said Juan impatiently, and glared at the prisoner. He pointed again, mumbling something.

'He says he didn't know there had been a fall of rock here,' said the guard. 'He says the entrance seems to be blocked up. But if you try to lift away some of these rocks, maybe you could find enough room to go in.'

Juan flew into a temper, but whether with the prisoner or the annoying fall of rocks it was difficult to say.

He fell upon the boulders and began to drag at them feverishly, shouting to Luis and Pepi to help. The prisoner at first did nothing but sat down miserably on a rock. Juan shouted at him too, and he dragged himself up to help, though he was too weak to do anything in the way of lifting.

He pulled at a rock, staggered and fell. The others let him lie where he fell, and went on dragging at the great stones, panting and wiping the sweat from their foreheads.

The two boys watched them. It looked impossible, from where they were, to unblock any cave entrance there. 'Why,' whispered Jack to Philip, 'hundreds of stones must have fallen there! They'll never, never be able to shift them like that!'

Evidently the men thought so too, after a while, for they gave up pulling the boulders about and sat down to rest. The guard pointed to the fallen prisoner and spoke.

'What about him? How are we going to take him back?'

'Oh, give him some food and a drink,' growled Juan. 'He'll be all right then.'

'We'd better go now,' whispered Philip. 'They'll be starting back soon. Come on. How disappointing that we haven't discovered anything, though! I did hope we might see something of the treasure.'

'If it's hidden behind that wall of fallen stone it'll need powerful machinery to get it out,' said Jack.

'Nobody could move those bigger stones by hand. Come on, quickly.'

They set out on their way back, going as quickly as they could, glad that they had marked rocks and trees or they might have missed their way here and there.

The girls welcomed them, and poured questions on them. But the boys shook their heads most disappointingly.

'The treasure cave is blocked up,' said Jack. 'I only hope the men don't give up and leave this valley altogether. We'll be properly stranded then.'

16

Rescue of the prisoner

Some while after Jack and Philip had got back to the cave, Lucy-Ann, who was looking out between the fern fronds, gave a cry. 'I say, there's a man down there! – look, by the waterfall! Two men – no, three!'

Jack pulled the string which tied back the fronds and let them swing together to hide the cave. Then, parting the fronds carefully, he looked through.

'I might have guessed they would come back this way, to have another hunt for us here,' he said. 'Blow them! One – two – three of them. Where's the prisoner?'

'Fallen by the way, I should think, poor fellow,' said Philip, peering out too. 'He looked terribly feeble.'

The children watched the three men eagerly to see what they meant to do. It was soon clear. Luis and Juan were to go back to their hut, but Pepi was to be left to keep watch on the waterfall, to see who went in and out, and to try and discover the way that was used. The children could not hear what was said, but it was all plain enough.

Luis and Juan departed. Where the prisoner was nobody could guess. Pepi sat down on a rock that over-looked the waterfall, just about the level of the ledge where the girls had stood the day before.

'Blow!' said Jack. 'How can we get in and out without being seen? It's true he's got his back to us, but he might turn round at any time.'

Lucy-Ann began to worry about the prisoner. 'Suppose he has fallen down on the way, and the men have left him there,' she said. 'He'd die, wouldn't he?'

'I suppose so,' said Jack, feeling anxious too.

'But Jack, we can't leave him to die,' said Lucy-Ann, her eyes big with horror. 'You know we can't. I shan't rest till I know what's happened to him.'

'I feel rather like that too,' said Jack, and the others nodded. 'There was something awful about the hopeless way he sat. I'm sure he was ill.'

'But how can we find out what's happened to him, whilst that fellow down there is guarding this place?' said Philip gloomily.

Everyone fell silent. It was a puzzler. Then Lucy-Ann brightened up. 'I know,' she said. 'There's one certain way of making sure Pepi doesn't see anyone creeping out of this cave.'

'What?' said Jack.

'Well, if one or two of us got behind the waterfall and

capered about a bit to attract the man's attention, he would be all eyes for them, and wouldn't notice anyone creeping out of this cave,' said Lucy-Ann.

'There's something in that,' said Jack, and Philip nodded. 'Yes, quite a good idea. Well, there's no time like the present. Shall we give a performance for dear Pepi now? You two girls could go and caper about, if you like – you are quite safe when you're behind the waterfall, because nobody can possibly get at you there, unless they go that same way as you do. And Pepi certainly doesn't know that way. Whilst you are attracting his attention, Philip and I will go off and see if we can see any sign of the prisoner.'

'Well, wait here till you see us behind the water,' said Dinah, and she got up. She and Lucy-Ann disappeared up the hole at the back of the cave. The boys waited patiently for them to appear behind the waterfall.

After some while Philip clutched Jack's arm. 'There they are! Good old Lucy-Ann, good old Dinah! They're having a fine old game down there. What are they waving? Oh, they've taken off their red pullovers and they're waving them like mad – doing a kind of dance.'

Pepi caught sight of them at once. He stared in surprise, and then stood up. He yelled and shouted and waved. The girls took no notice at all, but went on capering. Pepi began to try all kinds of ways to get to the waterfall.

'Now's our chance,' said Jack. 'Come on. His eyes will be glued on Lucy-Ann and Dinah for ages.'

They crept quickly out of the cave, swinging the fronds closely together behind them. They climbed up the rocks there and soon took cover so that they could not be seen. When the girls saw that they were safely out of the cave and could no longer be seen, they left the waterfall ledge and went back into the passage that led to the cave of echoes. They had done their bit.

The boys made their way cautiously over the rocks, keeping a good lookout for the others. When they were quite a long way from Pepi, they stopped to take counsel.

'Now – should we go back to that blocked up cave where apparently the treasure is, and see if we can find the prisoner fallen by the way – or shall we scout a bit in the other direction – back to the men's hut, to see if by any chance they've taken him there?'

'Better go to the men's hut,' said Philip, thinking. 'I don't think it's *very* likely they've left him to die by the wayside. They might still want to get something out of him.'

So they made their way back to the men's hut. How well they knew the way now! They saw the smoke of the fire long before they came near, and by that they knew the men were back.

There was no sign to be seen of the two men or of the prisoner. Cautiously the boys peered through the trees near the hut. The door of the hut was shut and presumably locked. Were the men inside?

'Hark, isn't that the sound of the plane's engine running?' asked Philip suddenly. 'Yes, it is. Are those fellows going off again?'

They went to a place from which they could see the plane well by means of Jack's field glasses. The men were not going off – merely doing something to their plane. There was no sign of the prisoner being with them.

'Stay here, Philip, with my field glasses and keep an eye on the plane and the men,' said Jack, pushing his glasses into Philip's hand. 'Come and tell me at once if they stop their work there and go towards the hut. I'm going to peep in at the hut window and see if the prisoner is there. I'm worried about him.'

'Right,' said Philip, and put the field glasses to his eyes. Jack sped off. He soon came to the hut. He tried the door. Yes, it was locked all right. He crept round to the window and peeped in.

The prisoner was there. He was sitting in the chair, the picture of misery, his face in his hands. As Jack looked, he heard him groan deeply, and it was such a dreadful noise that the boy's heart was wrung.

'If only I could get him out!' he thought. 'No use breaking the window. It's too small even for me to get in, and certainly that fellow couldn't squeeze out. What can I do? I can't break down the door. It's jolly strong!'

He went all round the hut two or three times, but

there was absolutely no way of getting in. He stood and stared at the door, hating it. Horrid strong thing!

And then he saw an unbelievable sight. There was a nail at one side of the door, and on it hung – a key! A large key! A key that surely must fit the door. Otherwise why should it be there? It must have been put there so that any of the men could go in and out at any time without waiting for the one who had the key.

With trembling fingers Jack took the key from the nail. He put it into the lock of the door. He turned it. It was stiff – but it turned all right.

The door swung open and Jack went in. The prisoner, hearing the door open, looked up. He stared in surprise at Jack. The boy grinned at him.

'I've come to set you free,' he said. 'Like to come with me?'

The man did not seem to understand. He frowned a little and stared even harder at Jack.

'Spik slow,' he said. Jack repeated what he had said. Then the boy tapped himself on the chest and said, 'I am your friend. Friend! Understand?'

The man evidently did understand that. A slow smile broke over his face. It was a nice face – a kindly, sad, trustable face, Jack thought. The boy held out his hand.

'Come with me,' he said.

The man shook his head. He pointed to his feet. They were bound tightly with rope, which the man obviously had not had the strength to untie. Jack whipped out his pocket-knife in a trice. He sawed through the thick strands and they fell apart. The man stood up unsteadily, looking as if he was about to fall. Jack steadied him, thinking that he would never be able to walk all the way to their cave. He seemed even weaker than before.

'Come on,' said the boy ugently. 'We haven't much time to lose.'

Jack put the cut pieces of rope into his pocket. He led the man to the door, put him outside and then carefully locked the door again, hanging the key on its nail. He grinned at the prisoner.

'Bit of a surprise for Juan and Luis to find you've apparently walked through a locked door,' said the boy. 'I'd like to be here when they unlock the door and find you gone.'

Jack took the man's arm and piloted him away into the cover of the nearby trees. The man walked very unsteadily. He gave a groan every now and again as if it hurt him to walk. Jack felt more and more certain that he would never be able to get to the cave.

He wondered what to do. Perhaps he could park the man in the old cowshed he and the others had found the first day they had arrived? He could put him in the last cowstall, and then fetch him the next day, when he was a little more recovered. That would be the best thing.

'You stay here a minute,' said the boy, thinking he had better run to Philip, tell him what had happened and get him to keep guard till he got the man safely installed in the shed.

Philip was intensely surprised to hear what Jack had to tell him. He nodded and agreed to stay on guard till Jack came for him.

'The men seem to be overhauling the plane,' he said. 'Looks as if they'll be busy for some time.'

Jack helped the stumbling prisoner over to the cow-shed. It took a long time to get there, because the man went so slowly.

Once there, he sank down in the stall and panted painfully. He was certainly an ill man. But there was no doctor for him – only Jack's gentleness, for which he seemed to be very grateful.

'You stay here till tomorrow, when I will fetch you to a safer hiding place,' said Jack, speaking very slowly indeed. 'I will leave you water to drink and food to eat.'

The boy meant to open a tin or two from the store still hidden in the bush. He could easily get them and leave them beside the man.

'The man tapped his chest. 'Otto Engler,' he said, and repeated it two or three times. Jack nodded, and pointed to his own chest.

'Jack Trent,' he said. 'Me Jack – you Otto.'

'Friend,' said the man. 'You – English?'

'Me English,' said Jack gravely. 'You?'

'Austrian,' said the man, pronouncing it in a curious way. 'Friend. Good friend. Why you here?'

Jack tried to explain how it was he and the others had come, but it was too complicated for the man to understand and he shook his head.

'Not understand,' he said. Then he leaned forward to Jack and spoke in a low voice.

'You know of treesure?'

'Treesure? Oh, you mean treasure,' said Jack, 'Not much. You know – of treasure?'

'I know all,' said the man. 'All! I draw you map – where treesure is. You good boy. I trust you.'

17

A treasure map

Jack's first feeling on hearing this was one of tremendous excitement. Then his face fell. He knew where the treasure was. Behind that fall of rock. What use was that? Nobody could get at it there.

'I know where treasure is,' said Jack, trying to speak slowly and simply. 'I saw you show the men this morning – but the rocks had fallen together, and they could not get into the treasure-cave behind.'

The man gave a short laugh. He seemed to understand. 'They are fools,' he said. 'Big fools. There is no treesure there.'

Jack stared at him. 'Do you mean to say – you fooled them?' he said. 'You knew that fall of rocks was there – and you took them to it, and pretended that the entrance to the treasure was all blocked up? Isn't the treasure behind those rocks after all?'

The man was frowning hard in his attempt to follow all that Jack was saying. He shook his head.

'No treesure there,' he said. 'I fool Juan and Pepi. Ah, ah, how they hurt their hands when they pull – so – at the rocks!'

Jack couldn't help grinning. What a fine trick to play! Well, then – where *was* the 'treesure'?

'I draw you map,' said Otto. 'And I tell you way out of valley too. By the Windy Pass. You will go that way, you and your friends, and you will take the map to a good friend of mine. It is time now to find the hidden treesure.'

'But why can't you come with us?' said Jack. 'Surely you could show us the way, Otto – the pass – and come to your good friend?'

'I am very ill man,' said Otto. 'If I do not get doctor and – how you say it? – middisin . . .'

'Yes, medicine,' said Jack.

'. . . middisin soon, I die,' said Otto. 'I have bad heart, very very bad. I get pain very bad. I not walk far now. So you take treesure map, you good boy, and you take pass out of valley, and go to Julius, my good friend. Then all will be well.'

'All right,' said Jack. 'I'm very sorry about you, Otto. Wish I could do something. I'll do my best to get to Julius quickly and bring back help to you. Do you think you might be able to walk to our hiding place tomorrow, and hide there whilst we go?'

'Pardon?' said Otto. 'You talk too quick, I not understand.'

Jack spoke more slowly. Otto nodded. He understood the second time.

'You leave me here today, and tomorrow perhaps I be strong enough to go with you to your place,' he said. 'We will see. If not, you must go through the pass and find Julius. I draw you map now, and I draw you also the way to the pass. Windy Pass. It is very, very narrow, but not difficult to, to . . .'

'To travel through?' said Jack. Otto nodded. He found a pencil and a notebook and began to draw. Jack watched him with interest. The waterfall appeared in the map. So did an oddly shaped rock. A bent tree came into the map, and a spring of water. Little arrows were drawn showing in what direction to go. It was really rather exciting.

Otto folded up the map. He gave it to Jack. 'Julius will know,' he said. 'He will read the map. Once he lived in the big farmhouse not far from here. But our enemies burnt it down, and all the other farms too, and took our cows and our horses, our pigs and everything we had. Many they killed, and only few of us escaped.'

'Now tell me the way to the pass,' said Jack.

Otto once more drew a map. The waterfall appeared in it. Jack put his finger on it.

'I know this water,' he said, speaking slowly so that Otto would understand. 'Our hiding place is near. Very near.'

'So!' said Otto, pleased. 'The way to the pass is above

the waterfall. You must climb to where it flows out of a hole in the mountainside. There – I have drawn you the way.'

'How shall we find Julius?' asked Jack.

'On the other side of the pass is a village, half burnt,' said Otto. 'You will ask anyone you meet to tell you where Julius is. They will know. Ah, Julius worked against the enemy all the time. Everyone knows Julius. He should be a great man now among his people – but times are strange and maybe he is no longer great, now that we have peace. But still, everyone knows Julius, and he will know what to do when you give him the treesure map. I will also write him a letter.'

Otto scribbled a short note, and gave that also to Jack. It was addressed to Julius Muller.

'Now you must leave me,' said Otto. 'You must go back to your friends. If I am better tomorrow I will come with you. But my heart is bad today, so bad. Always it pains me here.' He pressed his hand over his heart.

'Well, goodbye, and thank you,' said Jack, getting up. 'I do hope you will be safe here. There is meat for you, and tinned fruit, all ready opened. Well – so long till tomorrow.'

The man smiled a tired smile, sank back against the wall of the cowshed and closed his eyes. He was completely exhausted. Jack felt very sorry for him. He must get help as soon as he could, if Otto was not better by tomorrow. He and others would get out of the valley by the pass and go and find Julius at once, whoever he was. If he was a friend of Otto's, he might be able to get a doctor immediately.

Feeling much more cheerful about things, Jack went out of the cowshed. Golly, what would the others say when they knew he had the map of where the treasure-cave was to be found – and directions as to how to get out of the valley!

Philip came running up, out of breath. 'The men have just left the plane and are walking towards their hut,' he said. 'Come on, we'd better go. Is the prisoner safely in the shed?'

'Yes. Hope the men don't go there looking for him,' said Jack. 'Come on – let's get back to the girls. We shall have been away from them for ages.'

'We must look out for Pepi on the way back,' said Philip, as they set off. 'He may have got tired of watching the waterfall and the girls capering about, and have decided to cut back to the others.'

'I say – do you know what *I've* got?' said Jack, unable to keep the news to himself for a moment longer.

'What?' asked Philip.

'A map showing where the treasure is!' said Jack.

'But we know where it is,' said Philip. 'Behind that fall of rocks we saw this morning.'

'Well, it isn't!' said Jack triumphantly. 'The prisoner – his name's Otto – he fooled them properly. He pretended the treasure was in a cave behind the fall of rocks

– he knew the rocks had fallen, but he thought he could pretend he didn't know about them, and say the treasure was blocked by the landslide there. See?'

'Golly, and all the time the treasure was somewhere else!' said Philip. 'That was good work. Have you really got a map of the whereabouts of the treasure, Jack? And did you find out exactly what the treasure is?'

'No, I forgot to ask him that,' said Jack. 'But I found out an awful lot. I've got directions to find the pass that leads out of this valley – and a note to a man called Julius – and I know how these houses and things got burnt and why. Otto says if he's strong enough tomorrow he'll take us to the pass himself – but he gave me the maps in case he wasn't able to come with us. They're quite clear.'

This was really exciting news. Philip felt overjoyed. It looked as if they would be able to escape from the valley at last – and get help – and perhaps be in at the discovery of the treasure.

'Look out! – I believe I saw something moving over there,' whispered Jack suddenly, and the two boys crouched behind a bush. It was a good thing they did, for Pepi emerged from a thicket of trees and walked rapidly towards them. But it was obvious that he hadn't seen them.

Without a glance at their bush he strode on. 'I bet he's hungry and wants a meal,' grinned Jack. 'Good thing I spotted him. We'd have bumped right into him in two seconds. Well, that's good – we can hurry on now without being afraid of being seen. Gosh, I'm hungry!'

They both were. It was ages since they had had anything to eat. Thoughts of tinned salmon, sardines, tongue, apricots, peaches and pears floated before the mind's eye of both boys. They hurried as much as they could.

They were thankful when they pushed aside the fern fronds and saw the girls sitting in the cave behind. Dinah had got a fine meal ready and waiting.

'Good old Dinah!' cried Jack. 'I could almost give you a hug!'

Dinah grinned. 'Pepi's gone,' she said. 'Did you meet him?'

'Almost collided with him,' said Philip. 'Gosh, I could eat a whole tin of salmon by myself. How have things been with you and Lucy-Ann, Dinah? All right?'

'Very dull,' said Dinah. 'Nothing doing at all, except a few capers now and again behind the waterfall to keep Pepi interested. You should have seen his efforts to find the way up. Once Lucy-Ann and I really thought he had been swept away by the water. He slipped and fell, and disappeared for about twenty minutes. We were quite relieved when we saw him again.'

'What about you boys?' said Lucy-Ann. 'You look cheerful. Got good news? What about that poor prisoner?'

With their mouths full the boys told of all they had

done that day. The girls listened eagerly. When Jack fished the maps out of his pocket they fell on them with delight.

'A treasure map!' cried Lucy-Ann. 'I always wanted to see a real one. Oh, here's our waterfall, look! Surely the treasure isn't anywhere near it?'

'When are we going to find the treasure?' asked Dinah, her eyes shining.

'We're not going to,' said Jack, and her face fell at once. He explained why. 'We've got to get out of this valley, and find this fellow Julius. Apparently he will see to the unearthing of the treasure, whatever it is. Sorry to disappoint you, girls – but honestly, I do really think we ought to get out as quickly as we can, and let Aunt Allie and Bill know where we are. We should waste a lot of time looking for the treasure, and I think that now we've been told where to look for the pass out of the valley we ought to take it, and get help for ourselves and for poor old Otto too. He's a very ill man.'

It was clear that Jack was right. Dinah heaved a sigh of regret. 'I would so very much have liked to go and find that treasure,' she said. 'But never mind – perhaps this Julius man, whoever he is, will let us join the treasure-hunt with him. We might stay for that!'

It was now almost dark. The boys were tired out. They lay down on the 'bed' which Dinah had already made, feeling very sleepy. But the girls wanted to talk, and so did Kiki. They had had a very dull day. They chattered away, Kiki joining in, but the boys could hardly find the energy to answer.

'Kiki's been in and out of the cave of echoes today, yelling and squawking for all she was worth,' said Lucy-Ann. 'She's not afraid of the echoes any more. 'You should have heard the echoes when she did her express-train screech!'

'Jolly glad I didn't,' said Jack sleepily. 'Shut up, now, everyone. Get to sleep, because we've got an exciting day before us tomorrow, fetching Otto – and going to find the pass – and looking for Julius.'

'It looks as if this adventure is about to come to an end,' said Lucy-Ann.

But she was quite wrong. It wasn't anywhere *near* its end.

18

Now for Windy Pass!

Next morning the children peeped cautiously through the fern fronds to see if by any chance Pepi was on guard again. But there was no sign of him.

'I do wonder what Juan and Luis thought when they got back to their hut, unlocked it – and found the prisoner flown,' said Jack with a grin. 'They'll be astonished to find he went through a locked door.'

'Oh, they'll guess one of us rescued him,' said Dinah. 'Won't they be wild? I do hope they don't find him in that cowshed. He might tell tales of us.'

'He wouldn't,' said Jack at once. 'He's got a nice trustable face – rather like Bill's but not so strong.'

'I wish Bill would suddenly arrive here,' said Lucy-Ann with a sigh. 'I do really. I know we have managed things awfully well, but somehow when Bill comes along I feel really safe.'

'Well, you're safe enough now, aren't you?' demanded Jack. 'Didn't I find you a jolly good hiding place?'

'Yes, fine,' said Lucy-Ann. 'Oh, look, Philip – Kiki's after Lizzie!'

Lizzie had appeared down Philip's leg, and Kiki, who happened to be sitting near, had given a delighted squawk and pecked at her – but the lizard was a little too quick. She ran into Philip's shoe.

'Stop it, Kiki!' said Philip. 'Well – now we'd better get busy.'

'Busy Dizzy Lizzie,' said Kiki at once, and the children laughed.

'Really, Kiki's awfully clever at putting the same-sounding words together,' said Lucy-Ann. 'Busy Dizzy Lizzie – I'd never have thought of that. Clever Kiki!'

Kiki squawked and raised her crest high. She rocked herself from side to side, as she often did when she felt pleased with herself.

'Vain bird! Conceited bird!' said Jack, and scratched her poll. 'You leave Lizzie alone. She's about the most harmless pet Philip's ever had.'

'Well, she's better than those awful rats and mice and spiders and beetles and hedgehogs he's had running about him,' said Dinah with a shudder. 'I really quite like Lizzie, compared with them.'

'*Gracious!*' said Lucy-Ann, astonished. 'You *are* improving, Dinah!'

Lizzie and Kiki both joined in the breakfast the children had, though Kiki kept a sharp eye to see that Lizzie didn't take anything *she* wanted. When they had all finished they made their plans for the day.

'We'll fetch Otto first,' said Jack. 'Philip and I, I mean. No need for us all to go. Perhaps you two could pack up a few tins for us all to take with us when we go to look for the pass through the mountains. We shall want a meal on the way.'

'Right,' said Dinah. 'I hope you'll find Otto better. Then when you bring him here, we'll have a snack before we set out. Then over the pass we'll go, and find Julius – and somehow manage to send off a message to Mother and Bill. Maybe Bill will fly over in his plane . . .'

'And join the treasure hunt and let us help,' said Lucy-Ann. 'What a nice plan!'

It did seem a very nice one indeed. The boys set off, leaving Kiki behind with the girls. They went quickly over the mountain slope, keeping a good lookout, however, for Pepi and the others.

But they saw nobody. They made their way carefully to the cowshed. Jack left Philip on guard near by to give warning if anyone came near. Then he tiptoed to the shed and peeped in. There was no sound in there at all.

He could not see the last cowstall from where he stood. He walked softly in, stepping over the fallen rubble. He spoke softly.

'Otto! I'm back! Are you better?'

There was no reply. Jack wondered if the man was asleep. He made his way to the last stall.

It was empty. Otto was not there. Jack glanced round quickly. What could have happened?

The boy saw that the opened tins of meat and fruit that he had left for Otto were untouched. Otto had not eaten anything left for him. Why?

'Blow! Those men must have come looking for him when they found that he was gone from the hut,' thought Jack. 'And they found him here. Gosh! – what have they done with him? We'd better look out for ourselves, in case the men are on the watch for us. They'll know someone must have set Otto free, even if he has held his tongue about me.'

He went back to Philip. 'Otto's gone,' he said. 'Dare we have a squint at the hut? We might find out something then – what they've done with Otto, for instance.'

'Let's shin up that big tree we've climbed before,' said Philip. 'The one that we can see the plane from. If we saw all the men round about the plane, we'd know it was safe to go to the hut; but I don't feel inclined to run into danger if we think the men are by the hut. They might be watching for us to come again. If we're captured, the girls wouldn't know what to do.'

'All right. I'll climb the tree,' said Jack, and up he went, with Philip close behind him. He put his field glasses to his eyes to focus them on the plane – and then he gave a loud exclamation.

'Gosh! The plane's gone again! It isn't there!'

'No – it isn't,' said Philip in surprise. 'Well – *I* never heard it go this time, did you, Jack?'

'Well, I did think I heard a throbbing noise last night when I was half asleep,' said Jack. 'Yes, now I come to think of it, it must have been the plane I heard. Well, we've probably frightened the men away. They got the wind up when they knew other people were here – in a hiding place they couldn't find – people who rescued their prisoner.'

'Yes – and when they found they couldn't get at the treasure because a rock-fall had apparently blocked the entrance to it, I suppose they thought it wasn't much use staying,' said Philip. 'So they've gone. Thank goodness! Now we can go back to the girls, and shoot off to the pass quickly. To tell you the truth, I was a bit worried about taking Otto with us, because from what you said it didn't sound as if we'd be able to go very fast with him. And if he'd had a heart attack by the way we wouldn't have known what to do.'

'I wonder where they've taken him to,' said Jack. 'Let's hope that now they find they can't get any more out of him they've taken him back to where he belongs, and will get a doctor to him.'

They climbed down the tree, and set off back to the girls as fast as they could. Now for the pass.

The girls were most surprised to see the two boys back so soon – but they were even more surprised to see they were alone.

'Where's Otto?' asked Dinah.

'Down the well,' said Kiki. Nobody took any notice of her and she screeched.

Jack explained. 'The plane's gone – and Otto's gone – so I suppose they've all gone off, disgusted at not being able to get at the treasure. Good riddance to them!'

'Hear! hear!' said Dinah, very much relieved to know that their enemies were safely out of the way. 'Well, what are we going to do now?'

'Go and look for the pass,' said Jack. 'I've got the map Otto drew. What a mercy he gave it to me! We'd never find the pass by ourselves without a map, I'm sure of that. I mean, the pass out of these mountains might be anywhere. Apparently there *is* only one pass, and that's this one – the Windy Pass. Come on, let's go. Packed up a few tins, Dinah?'

'Yes,' said Dinah. 'Now, where do we go from here? Up or down?'

'Up,' said Philip, poring over the map that Jack took from his pocket. 'Up – to where the waterfall begins – here, look. Then we go along a rocky ledge – see, Otto's drawn it – then we come to a thick wood, look – and then up a steep bit to another ledge. Then we come to a proper road – the pass road that I suppose all the people of the valley used when they wanted to leave this district and visit another. Once we're on that road I shall feel better.'

'So shall I,' said Dinah fervently. 'It will be nice to see a *road*. We might even see somebody walking on it.'

'Shouldn't think so, as we haven't seen anyone in this valley at all except ourselves and the men,' said Jack. 'It strikes me as a bit queer, I must say, to think that although there's a perfectly good pass in and out of this lovely valley, it appears to be quite deserted. I wonder why.'

'Oh, I expect there's a good reason,' said Dinah. 'Come on, do let's go. The first part will be easy, because we've only got to keep near the waterfall.'

But it wasn't quite so easy as she thought, for the mountain cliff was exceedingly steep there, and the children had to do a lot of stiff climbing. Still, they managed it, for their legs were well used to walking and climbing by now.

The waterfall roared by them all the way. It made a terrific noise as it fell, and Lucy-Ann thought how nice it would be when they reached the top and didn't have to listen to quite such a colossal din.

After some time they came to where the waterfall began. It gushed out of a great hole in the mountainside and fell sheerly down, tumbling against huge rocks on the way. It was really a marvellous sight to see.

'Goodness, it does give me a funny feeling to see that great mass of water coming out of the mountain,' said Lucy-Ann, sitting down. 'It's so *sudden*, somehow.'

'I suppose when the snows melt, and the rain pours

down, there is a terrific amount of water soaking down into the mountaintop,' said Jack. 'And it all collects and has to get out somehow. This is one way it gets out – through this hole – making a tremendous waterfall.'

'Where do we go now?' asked Dinah, who was very impatient to get out of the valley.

'We go up on that rocky ledge,' said Jack. 'Golly, it looks a bit narrow – it runs right over the waterfall! Lucy-Ann, don't you dare look down, in case you feel giddy.'

'I don't much feel as if I want to walk along there,' said poor Lucy-Ann.

'I'll help you,' said Jack. 'You'll be all right as long as you don't look down.'

They went along the rocky ledge quite safely, Lucy-Ann holding tightly to Jack's hand. Kiki flew above their heads, squawking encouragement.

'See how they run, see how they run!' she called, having apparently remembered the second line of 'Three Blind Mice.'

Lucy-Ann gave a giggle. 'We're not exactly running, Kiki,' she said. 'Oh, thank goodness the ledge has come to an end. Now we go through that wood, don't we?'

Jack looked at his map. 'Yes – apparently we go straight through. Where's my compass? I'll set it so that we walk in a straight line in the direction Otto has put on his map.'

They entered the wood. It was a pine wood, rather

dark and silent. Nothing grew under the tall pine-trees. The wind blew them and they made a loud whispering noise, which upset Kiki.

'Sh!' she called. 'Shhhhhhhhhh!'

'Here's the end of the wood!' called Jack. 'Now for another steep bit to another ledge – and we'll look down on the road. Come on, everybody!'

19

A great disappointment – and a plan

It certainly was a stiff climb again, up the steep, rather stony slope to the ledge they could see some way above. Lucy-Ann almost cried because her feet kept slipping so.

'I take one step up, and slip two steps back,' she wailed.

'Well, hang on to me then,' said Philip, and gave her a tug up each time she took a step.

They all wanted a rest when they came to the next ledge, and to their delight they saw a patch of wild raspberries growing there. They could sit down in the canes and feast as they rested. Lovely! Kiki liked the raspberries very much indeed, and ate so many that Jack called to her.

'Kiki! You'll go pop!'

'Pop goes the weasel,' answered Kiki, and helped herself to a few dozen more raspberries.

Soon they all felt they could go on again. They were very high up now, and could see even more mountains towering behind the ones they knew. It was a most magnificent sight.

'I feel very small and lost somehow, with all those great mountains sitting there,' said Lucy-Ann, and the others felt the same. 'Come on – let's go round the ledge now. We shall soon see the road. Thank goodness this ledge isn't narrow. It's almost wide enough to take a car.'

It was not so easy walking round the ledge as Lucy-Ann thought, however, for there had been a fall of rocks there, further along, and there was a good deal of scrambling about to be done. They were thankful when they had got over the rock-fall and come to smoother ground again.

The ledge rounded a bend in the mountainside, and then, quite suddenly, the children saw the road below them. Yes, it was really a road! They stood and looked at it in delight.

'I never thought I should be so pleased to see a road again,' said Dinah. 'The road out of the valley! The road to Somewhere at last!'

'Look,' said Lucy-Ann, 'it winds up from quite a long way down. We can't see where it goes to from here, because it's hidden round the bend.'

'You can see the pass, the Windy Pass, from here, though,' said Jack, pointing. 'See where this mountain and the next almost touch? That's where the pass must be – fairly high up and awfully narrow. I bet we'll have to go through it in single file.'

'No, we won't,' said Philip scornfully. 'It's bound to be wide enough to take a cart. It only looks narrow because we're far off.'

'Come on, let's get down to the road,' said Dinah, and began to climb down to it. They were about twenty feet above it.

'I say, isn't it overgrown with grass and weeds!' said Jack, astonished. 'That shows how little it has been used lately. Strange, isn't it? You'd think the people would put their only road out of the valley into some sort of order.'

'It's jolly peculiar, *I* think,' said Philip. 'Come on – we can at least see it's a road, even if it is overgrown with weeds.'

They walked along the road for some way. It wound upwards always, following long curves in and out on the slopes of the mountain. At last the children could clearly see where the Windy Pass must be, a narrow passage between the two mountains, theirs and the next.

It was cold so high up and the wind was very strong. If the children had not been warm with climbing they would have shivered. As it was, they were all as warm as toast.

'Now – round this next corner – and I bet we shall see the pass!' cried Jack. 'Then hurrah for the way out of this mysterious valley!'

They rounded the corner. Yes – there lay the pass – or what must once have been the pass. But it was a pass no longer.

Something had happened. The narrow way between the great mountains was blocked high with great rocks and black boulders. It was impassable.

At first the four children didn't quite take it in. They stood and stared in wonder.

'What's happened there?' said Jack at last. 'It looks like an earthquake or something. Did you ever see such a terrible mess?'

'Great holes have been blown in the rocky walls on either side of the pass,' said Philip. 'Look, even high up there are holes like craters.'

They stared in silence, and then Jack turned to the others. 'Do you know what I think has happened?' he said. 'Well, when enemies were here, fighting, they bombed the pass – and blocked it. All that devastation has been caused by bombs – I'm sure it has.'

'Yes, I think you're right, Jack,' said Philip. 'It's just what it looks like. Aeroplanes must have flown just over the pass, and dropped scores of bombs on the narrow road there. It's absolutely impassable.'

'Do you mean – we can't get out?' asked Lucy-Ann in a trembling voice. Philip nodded.

'Afraid so,' he said. 'Nobody could get over that steep, high, dangerous wall of blown up rocks. This explains why people haven't come along to live in this valley yet. I suppose most of those living here were killed, and the rest escaped over the pass. Then it was blown up and nobody could come back. Those men in the plane, Juan and the rest, must have got wind of some treasure hidden in the valley, and thought they would try to enter the place by plane. About the only way to enter it too.'

Lucy-Ann sat down and cried. 'I'm so disappointed,' she wailed. 'I thought we were going to escape from this horrid, lonely valley, I really did. But now we're still prisoners here – and n-n-n-nobody can come in to rescue us!'

The others sat down by Lucy-Ann, feeling rather desperate too. They stared hopelessly at the blocked pass. What a terrible blow! Just as they had so hoped they would be able to escape, and get to Julius, and tell him about the treasure.

'Let's have something to eat,' suggested Dinah. 'We'll feel better then. No wonder we feel a bit dumpy now.'

'Humpy dumpy,' said Kiki at once. That made them laugh.

'Idiot!' said Philip. '*You* don't care about a blocked up pass, do you, Kiki? You could fly over. It's a pity we can't tie a message to your leg and send you over to Julius for help.'

'Oooh – couldn't we do that?' said Lucy-Ann at once.

'No, silly! For one thing, Kiki would probably tear the message off her leg,' said Jack, 'and for another she'd never know who to go and look for. She's a clever bird, but not as clever as that.'

They felt a lot better after their meal. They ate it with

their backs to the blocked pass. Nobody could bear to look at it.

'I suppose we'll have to go back to our cave,' said Dinah at last. 'Doesn't seem anything else to do really.'

'No, I suppose there isn't,' said Jack rather gloomily. 'What a sell, isn't it?'

They had a good long rest. The sun was very fierce, but the wind was so strong that they were never too hot. In fact Lucy-Ann went to a rock that sheltered her from the wind, because she felt too cool.

They started back after their rest. They were not nearly so cheerful and talkative as when they had set out that morning. The thought of having to stay in the lonely valley, after having such high hopes of escaping, was very damping to all of them.

Lucy-Ann looked so miserable that Jack tried to think of something to cheer her up. He thought of something really startling.

'Cheer up, Lucy-Ann,' he said. 'Maybe we'll find the treasure now, to make up for our disappointment.'

Lucy-Ann stopped and stared at him, thrilled. '*Really?*' she said. 'Oh, *Jack* – yes, let's look for the treasure ourselves now!'

Everyone stopped and thought about it for a few exciting moments. 'Well, why not?' said Philip. 'We can't get word about it to Julius, because we can't get over the pass. Those men have gone, and Otto is gone too. There's only us left. We might as well hunt for the treasure. It would be something exciting to do, to pass away the time.'

'How simply gorgeous!' cried Dinah. 'Just what I've always wanted to do – hunt for treasure. When shall we start? Tomorrow?'

'I say – suppose we really found it!' said Philip, looking thrilled. 'Should we get a share of it, I wonder?'

'What a good thing Otto gave you the map, Freckles!' said Dinah to Jack. She always called him Freckles when she felt in a very good humour. 'Let's have a look at it.'

Jack took it out of his pocket. He unfolded the sheet of paper and spread it out. Otto had marked it with compass directions, just as he had marked the map showing the way to the pass.

'See the things he has drawn or printed,' said Jack. 'See this funny shaped rock – it's shaped like a man in a cloak, with a ball-like head. If we saw that rock, we'd know it was a signpost to the treasure.'

'And what's this – a bent tree?' asked Dinah. 'Yes, but how are we to know where to look for them? We can't go wandering all over the mountainside looking for queer-shaped rocks and bent trees and things.'

'Of course not,' said Jack. 'We'd have to begin properly, from the beginning – and the beginning is the waterfall we know. Otto drew a path from where the cowshed is to the waterfall, see – well, we can start right *at* the waterfall without bothering about the path. Then, from the top of the fall we must look for that bent tree, and walk to there. Then from the bent tree we look for this – let's see, what did he say that was? – oh yes, it's a stretch of smooth black rock – well, when we get there, we look next for a spring of water – and from there we look out for that funny shaped rock. Then somewhere about there is the treasure.'

'Golly!' said Lucy-Ann, her eyes nearly popping out of her head. 'Let's get back to the waterfall and start straight away. Come on!'

Jack folded up the map and looked round at the three excited faces. He grinned. 'The treasure won't be much use to us, cooped up in this valley as we are,' he said. 'But it will be something really thrilling to do.'

They set off once again, their minds busy with treasure hunting. If only they could find what those men had been looking for and had not found! What would Bill say? He would wish to goodness he had been with them. He always said they fell into adventure after adventure.

When they got back to the waterfall, the sun had gone in, and huge black clouds hung over their mountain. Enormous drops of rain began to fall. The children gazed in disappointment at the lowering sky.

'Blow! said Philip. 'There's going to be a rain storm, I should think. No good going off treasure hunting in this. Better get into the cave before we get soaked. Here comes the rain properly!'

They only just got into their cosy cave in time. Then

the rain pelted down in torrents, and added its voice to the roar of the waterfall.

'Rain all you like!' called Jack. 'But do be sunny tomorrow – we're going treasure hunting!'

20

Signposts to the treasure

They slept very soundly indeed that night, for they were tired out. The rain fell all night long, but towards dawn the clouds cleared away, and the sky, when the sun rose, was a clear pale blue. Lucy-Ann liked it very much when she parted the soaking fern fronds and looked out.

'Everything's newly washed and clean, even the sky,' she said. 'Lovely! Just look!'

'Just the day for a treasure hunt,' said Jack. 'I hope this sun will dry the grass quickly, or we shall get our feet soaked.'

'Good thing we brought so many tins out of the men's hut,' said Dinah, reaching down two or three. 'Are there still some in that bush where we first hid them, Jack?'

'Plenty,' said Jack. 'I took one or two to open for Otto the day before yesterday, but there are heaps left. We can go and get them some time.'

They tied back the fern fronds and ate their breakfast

sitting at the front of the cave, looking out on the far mountains, backed by the sky, which was now turning a deeper blue.

'Well, shall we set off?' said Jack, when they had finished. 'Kiki, take your head out of that tin. You know it's completely empty.'

'Poor Kiki!' said Kiki. 'What a pity!'

They all scrambled out of the cave. Things were certainly drying fast in the hot summer sun. 'Look, those rocks are steaming!' said Lucy-Ann in surprise, pointing to some nearby rocks. So they were. They looked most peculiar with the steam rising up.

'Better take some food with us,' said Jack. 'Got some, Dinah?'

'Of course,' said Dinah. 'We can't come all the way back here for food.'

'We've got to get to where the waterfall begins, just as we did yesterday,' said Jack. 'Follow me, all of you. I know the way.'

They soon stood at the top of the waterfall, and once more watched the great gush of water surge out from the heart of the mountain. It seemed twice as big and turbulent as the day before.

'Well, I suppose the underground water has been swelled up because of last night's rain,' said Philip. 'And so the waterfall is bigger and stronger.'

'Yes, that's the reason,' said Jack, raising his voice to a

shout because of the noise of the water. 'Kiki, stop screeching in my ear.'

The waterfall excited Kiki, and she made a terrible noise that morning. Jack would not have her on his shoulder after a while, because of her screeches. She flew off in a huff.

'Now, what about that bent tree?' said Dinah, remembering. By this time they were standing a little way above the beginning of the waterfall. 'I can't see any bent tree at all!'

'Oh, golly – don't say there isn't a bent tree!' groaned Jack, looking this way and that, all round and about and above his head. 'Gosh, there doesn't seem to be one, does there?'

There didn't. What few trees they could see were perfectly straight. Then Lucy-Ann gave a cry and pointed downwards. 'There it is, isn't it? – just below us, on the other side of the waterfall. Look!'

They all went to stand by Lucy-Ann, and looked. She was right. On the other side of the fall, some way below them, was a curiously bent tree. It was a birch tree, and why it should have grown so bent over was a puzzle. The wind was no stronger there than anywhere else. Anyway, it was decidedly bent and that was all that mattered.

They crossed above the beginning of the waterfall, clambering over the rocks, and then scrambled down on the other side of the fall. They reached the bent tree at last.

'First signpost,' said Jack.

'No second,' said Dinah. 'The waterfall is really the first.'

'Well, second then,' said Jack. 'Now for the third – a big stretch of flat black rock – a wall of it, I should think.'

They all looked in every direction for a stretch of black rock. This time it was Jack's keen eyes that spotted it. It was some way off, and looked difficult to reach, for it meant climbing along the steep face of the mountainside, which just there was very cliff-like.

Still, it had to be done, so they set off. It was easier after the first stretch, for there were all kinds of plants and bushes firmly rooted in the sloping cliff, and these could be used as handholds or footholds. Jack helped Lucy-Ann along, but Dinah scorned Philip's help, especially as she knew he had the lizard somewhere about him.

It took them at least half an hour of stiff scrambling and climbing to reach the wall of black rock, though actually, in distance, it was not so very far. They stood by the rock, panting.

'Funny shiny black rock,' said Jack, running his fingers over the smooth surface. 'Wonder what it is.'

'Oh, never mind,' said Dinah, impatient to get on. 'What's our next signpost? This is the third.'

'A spring of water,' said Philip. 'Isn't that right, Jack – or shall we look at the map?'

'No – I know it by heart,' said Jack. 'A spring of water is next. Not that I can see one at all – though I wish I could because I could do with a drink after that hot scramble. My hands are filthy, and so are my knees.'

'Yes, we could all do with a jolly good wash now,' said Philip. 'A good old rub and a scrub.'

'Rubbenascrub,' said Kiki, and went off into one of her dreadful cackles.

'Stop it, Kiki,' said Jack. 'I'll give *you* a rubbenascrub in a minute.'

There was no spring of water to be seen. Lucy-Ann began to look very disappointed.

'Cheer up!' said Jack. 'We may not be able to *see* the spring from this wall of rock – but we can surely find it if it's anywhere near.'

'Let's listen,' suggested Dinah.

So they stood perfectly still and listened. 'Shhhhhh!' said Kiki annoyingly.

Jack smacked her on the beak. She gave a dismal squawk and sat silent. And, in the silence of the peaceful mountainside, the children heard the tinkle-tinkle of water – a merry, gurgling noise, cheerful and friendly.

'I can hear it!' cried Lucy-Ann in delight. 'It comes from somewhere over there.'

She leapt across to a little thicket of trees, and there, hidden deep in the flower-strewn grass, bubbled a clear spring, trickling down the hillside, a tiny stream of crystal cold water.

'It starts just up there, look,' said Jack, and pointed to a big bush. The spring bubbled out from below the bush. 'Fourth signpost!'

'Now for the fifth – and last!' said Lucy-Ann excited. 'Oooh – do you honestly think we are getting near to the treasure? It's really not *very* far from our waterfall cave. I thought I could hear the faint, distant roar of the fall when I stood listening for the gurgling of the spring.'

'I thought I could too,' said Dinah. 'Now, what do we look for next?'

'The oddly shaped rock,' said Jack. 'You know – like a man in a long cloak, with a round head at the top.'

'Easy!' said Philip triumphantly, and pointed upwards. 'There it is – quite clear against the sky!'

They all looked up. Philip was right. There stood the curious-shaped rock, easy to see against the sky.

'Come on!' said Jack excitedly. 'Up we go! Come along, treasure hunters!'

They climbed up to where the odd-shaped rock stood. Other rocks lay about, but this one was much taller, and, because of its height and shape, it stood out among the others.

'Our last signpost!' said Jack. 'And now – where's the treasure?'

Ah, yes – where was the treasure? Lucy-Ann looked about the hillside as if she half expected it to be strewn there. The others began to search for a cave opening. But nobody could find anything.

'Why didn't you ask Otto exactly where to find the treasure, after coming to the last signpost?' complained Dinah, tired and disappointed, coming over to Jack.

'Well, I didn't know *we* were going to look for it, silly, did I?' said Jack. 'I thought Julius Muller was going to take charge of the treasure hunt. No doubt if he got as far as this he'd know where the treasure was all right.'

'Well, it's most awfully disappointing to come all this way, and read the map so well, and then not find a thing,' said Dinah, who was cross and tired. 'I'm fed up. I shan't hunt any more. You can all go on looking if you like, but I'm going to have a rest.'

She flung herself down, and lay flat, looking upwards at the steep mountainside above her. It was ridged with flat slabs of rock, sticking out here and there like ledges. Dinah examined them lazily with her eyes. Then she sat up suddenly.

'Hi!' she called to the others. 'Look up there!'

They came over to her and looked up. 'See those big ledges of rock sticking out all the way up the cliff-side?' she said. 'Like shelves. Well, look halfway up – see one that sticks out rather far? Look underneath it. Is that a hole there?'

'It does look rather like a hole,' said Jack. 'Maybe a fox-hole, though. Still, it's the only sizeable hole hereabouts, so we'd better explore. I'll go up. Coming, Tufty?'

'Rather,' said Philip. 'It doesn't look difficult. Aren't you two girls coming too?'

Dinah forgot that she was fed up, and she joined in the climb to the hole under the ledge of rock. When they got there they found that it was a very big hole indeed. It could not possibly be seen from above, for the shelf of rock stuck right out over it and hid it. It could only be seen from one place below, at a certain angle – and that was the place where Dinah had flung herself down some time back.

'Bit of luck you happened to spot it, Dinah,' said Jack. 'We might have hunted all day and never found it. I wonder if this is the entrance to the *real* treasure cave.'

They peered down. The hole yawned below them, dark and appearing rather vast. 'Where's my torch?' said Jack, and, taking it from his pocket, he switched it on.

The children gazed down into the hole. It seemed nothing but a hole. No treasure was there. But, as Jack swung his torch a little further down, Dinah thought she caught sight of a passage further back.

'I believe,' she said, almost falling into the hole in her excitement, 'I do believe it goes right back, into a passage.'

Kiki flew off Jack's shoulder and disappeared into the hole. A mournful voice floated up to them.

'What's down there, Kiki?' called Jack.

'Three blind mice,' answered Kiki, solemnly and untruthfully. 'Three blind mice. Pop!'

'You're a fibber,' said Jack. 'Anyway – down we go to find the . . .'

'Three blind mice,' said Kiki, and went off into an imitation of Lucy-Ann's giggle.

21

The strange caves

Jack went down the hole first. He lowered himself right in, and only had to drop about a foot to the ground below.

'Lucy-Ann, you come next,' he said, and helped her down. Then came the others, excited and eager. Had they really found the treasure cave?

'It simply must be the hiding place for the treasure!' said Jack. 'There isn't another hole or cave anywhere. Now, let me flash my torch round a bit.'

At the back of the hole, as Dinah had thought, there was a passage – quite a wide one, and fairly high. A very tall man could have walked down it with ease.

'Come on!' said Jack, his voice shaking with excitement. 'We're getting warm!'

They followed him down the passage, Kiki sitting on his shoulder. Lucy-Ann held on to his sleeve, half fearful of what they might find.

The passage was wide and high all the way along, but

wound about a little. It went downwards, and kept more or less in the same direction, for all its windings – that is, towards the heart of the mountain.

Suddenly the passage came to an abrupt end. Jack paused, and gasped. In front of him was a most extraordinary sight.

His torch shone brightly on to an unending mass of brilliant columns, hanging from the high roof of a cave. Whatever could they be?

Lucy-Ann clutched his arm and gasped too. She stared at the shining white things. She saw that other white columns were growing up from the floor of the cave too. Some had met the hanging ones, and had joined, so that it seemed as if the cave roof was being supported by pillars.

'Jack! What is it? Is it the treasure?' whispered Lucy-Ann.

'It's icicles, isn't it?' said Dinah in an awed tone. 'I've never seen anything so beautiful in my life! Look at them hanging down – so still and white and lovely!'

'No – they're not icicles,' said Jack. 'They are stalactites – at least, the hanging ones are. They're not made of ice, either – but of limestone, I think. My word – what a sight!'

The children stood quite still and gazed their fill at the silent, beautiful cave. Its roof was as high as a cathedral, and the graceful stalactites hung down from it in dozens, gleaming in the light of Jack's torch.

'The ones growing up from the floor are stalagmites, I think,' said Jack. 'Aren't they, Philip? Do you know anything about them? I've never in my life seen anything like this before!'

'Yes – they're stalagmites,' said Philip. 'I remember seeing pictures of them. Stalactites and stalagmites. Gosh, what a sight!'

Kiki tried to say the two words and couldn't. Even she seemed to be awed by the amazing and unexpected discovery.

'Oh, look!' said Lucy-Ann suddenly, and pointed to what looked like an old, old shawl carved in ivory. 'Look – this has grown here too – it's just like a shawl – even to the pattern in it! And look at that sort of gate over there – all carved too! Surely somebody made them – surely they didn't just grow!'

'Well – they *formed*,' said Jack, trying to explain. 'You know – just as the crystals in a snowflake form. They don't grow because they're not alive – they *form*.'

Lucy-Ann couldn't quite understand. Secretly she thought that all the marvellous hanging pillars had grown, and then got frozen in their beauty.

I thought this must be the treasure!' she said, half laughing.

'I'm not surprised,' said Jack. 'It's too beautiful for words. Fancy finding a cave like this! It's like an enormous underground cathedral – it just wants an organ to begin playing a grand and magnificent hymn.'

'There's a kind of path down the middle,' said Dinah. 'I don't know if it's just a natural path, Jack, or whether it has been made by man. Do you see what I mean?'

'Yes,' said Jack, flashing his torch along it. 'Bit of both, I think. Well – shall we go on? There's no treasure here.'

They went along the middle of the great silent hall, surrounded on all sides by the hanging icicle-like pillars. Lucy-Ann pointed out many that had joined with columns growing from the ground.

'The drops of water from the stalactites must have dripped to the ground, and made stalagmites form there, growing up to meet the column above,' said Philip. 'They must have taken ages and ages to form – hundreds of years. I say – no wonder this cave feels awfully old to us. I feel as if there is no Time here at all – no years, or days of the week or hours – just nothing.'

Lucy-Ann didn't like that very much. It gave her a strange feeling of being only a dream, and not real. She took hold of Jack's arm and was glad to feel its nice, solid warmth.

They walked slowly to the end of the enormous cave. A great archway stood there, and that too was set with stalactites, which, however, did not hang far down. The children could walk under them with ease.

'This archway is quite like a tunnel,' said Philip. His voice sounded big and hollow there and made them all jump. Kiki gave a mournful cough, which was magnified to a hollow, giant cough that startled everyone very much.

They came to another cave. The roof of this was not so high as the one before, and only small, icicle-like stalactites hung from it.

'Do those stalactites shine in the dark?' asked Dinah suddenly. 'I thought I saw something glowing in the corner over there.'

Jack switched off his torch – and immediately the children gasped. For up in the roof and over the walls there glowed thousands of tiny stars. They were green and blue, and shone and flickered in a most enchanting manner.

'Gracious! What are they?' whispered Dinah, amazed. 'Are they alive?'

The boys didn't know. They watched the shimmering flickering stars, that seemed to go in and out like elfin lights. 'Might be a kind of glowworm,' said Jack. 'Aren't they lovely?'

He put on his torch again and the roof shone brightly in the yellow-white light. The stars disappeared.

'Oh, do put your torch out!' begged Lucy-Ann. 'I want to watch those stars a bit longer. I never saw anything so fascinating in my life! They shine like phosphorescence – all blue and green and green and blue; look how they flicker off and on. Oh, I wish I could take a hundred back with me and put them on my bedroom ceiling at home!'

The others laughed, but they too thought that the shining, flickering stars were most entrancing to watch. Jack did not put on his torch again until each had gazed his fill.

'That's two simply wonderful caves,' said Lucy-Ann with a sigh. 'What will the next one be? I really do feel as if we'd discovered Aladdin's Cave, or something like that!'

A long passage, leading downwards, led out of the cave of stars, as Lucy-Ann named it.

'We found a cave of echoes, a cave of stalactites and a cave of stars,' she said. 'I like this part of our adventure. Now I'd like to find a cave of treasure.'

The tunnel they were in was wide and high like the first passage they had entered. Jack's torch suddenly shone brightly on something on the floor. He stopped.

'Look at that!' he said. 'What is it?'

Dinah bent to pick it up. 'It's a brooch,' she said. 'A brooch without its pin. The pin's gone. It must have broken and the brooch fell off whoever was wearing it. Isn't it perfectly lovely?'

It certainly was. It was a large gold brooch, about three inches wide, set with brilliant red stones, as red as blood.

'Are they rubies?' said Dinah in awe. 'Look how they glow! Oh, Jack, do you think this is a bit of the treasure?'

'Probably,' said Jack, and at once excitement caught hold of the children again, and their hearts began to beat fast. A ruby brooch, set in carved gold! What would the other treasure be? Wonderful visions arose in the children's minds and they stumbled on their way eagerly, their eyes searching the ground for any other gleaming jewel.

'If we could find a cave of jewels,' said Lucy-Ann. 'Oooooh – all gleaming like stars and suns! That's what I would love.'

'We might find something like that,' said Dinah. 'If we do, I shall deck myself from head to foot with them and pretend I'm a princess.'

The passage went on and on, still leading downwards, but, when Jack looked at his compass, he saw that he was no longer going into the heart of the mountain, but in the opposite direction. He hoped they wouldn't suddenly come out into the daylight without finding the cave of treasure.

Suddenly they came to steps that led downwards. They were carved out of the solid rock, steep, wide steps that curved as the passage curved.

'Almost a spiral stairway,' said Jack. 'Where are we coming to now?'

There were about twenty of the steps. Then came an enormous door, made of some kind of stout wood, set with iron studs. The children stood and stared at it.

A door! What was behind it? Was it locked and bolted? Who had put it there, and why? Was it to shut in the treasure cave and guard it?

There was no handle to turn. There was not even a lock to be seen. There were great bolts, but these were not shot into place.

'How can you open a door without a handle?' said Jack in despair. He pushed at the door, but it remained quite firm.

'Kick it, like we did the door of the hut,' said Philip, and Jack kicked it hard. But the door did not open.

They stared at it in despair. To come so far and then to be stopped by a door! It was too bad. Jack shone his torch all over the door, from top to bottom.

Lucy-Ann's sharp eyes noticed something. 'See that iron stud?' she said, pointing. 'It's much brighter than the others. I wonder why.'

Jack shone his torch on it, and saw that it was slightly bigger than the others – and also, as Lucy-Ann said, it was brighter, as if it had had some handling.

He pressed it. Nothing happened. He banged on it with a stone. No result at all.

'Let *me* try,' said Philip, and pushed Jack aside. 'Shine your torch on it closely. That's right.'

Philip took hold of the iron stud and shook it. It seemed to give a little. He shook it again. Nothing happened. Then he thought of twisting it.

It twisted round very easily indeed. There was a loud click – and the door swung slowly open. Jack switched off his torch, afraid that anyone in the cave might see them – though if anyone had been there surely they would have heard the bangs and kicks at the door.

The door now stood wide open. A dim light shone beyond, showing another cave. Lucy-Ann clutched Jack's arm in fright.

'It's full of people,' she whispered. 'Look!'

22

The treasure at last!

The four children stared breathlessly through the open door. They saw something that made them feel very creepy.

In the dim light figures stood about all over the place. Their eyes gleamed queerly, and their teeth shone in the darkness. Their arms and necks flashed and glittered with jewels.

The children clutched one another in fright. Who were these strange, silent folk, standing about with gleaming eyes, covered with jewels?

The people in the cave did not move. They did not speak a word either. Not one of them was sitting. All were standing. They stood there, some turned towards the frightened children, some turned away. Why didn't they speak? Why didn't they point to the children and say, 'Look – who's there?'

Lucy-Ann began to shiver. 'Let's go back. I don't like them. They're not alive. Only their eyes are.'

Kiki suddenly gave a squawk, left Jack's shoulder, and flew to the shoulder of one of the nearby figures, a woman dressed in clothes that glowed richly in the half-light of the cave.

Still the woman did not move. How strange! The children suddenly felt much better when they saw that Kiki did not seem in the least afraid of the queer company.

'Polly put the kettle on,' said Kiki, and pecked at the hair of the woman he was sitting on.

The children held their breath again. What would the woman do to Kiki – enchant her with her strange eyes, cast a spell on her and turn her into stone? Perhaps all these people had been turned into stone?

'Let's go back,' said Lucy-Ann urgently. 'I don't like this cave. I don't like these people, or their horrid gleaming eyes.'

Jack suddenly jumped down the step that was below the great open door. He marched boldly into the silent cave. Lucy-Ann squealed and tried to catch his sleeve.

Jack walked right up to the woman on whose shoulder Kiki sat. He peered closely at her. He looked into her wide open glittering eyes. He touched her hair. Then he turned to the horrified children.

'What do you think? She's a statue – all dressed up beautifully – with real hair – and jewels for eyes! What do you think of that?'

The others could not believe it – but they were very

thankful to hear Jack's words, and to see him wandering among the crowd of still figures, apparently quite unharmed.

Philip and Dinah stepped down into the cave of figures too, but Lucy-Ann still did not quite dare to. She watched the others looking at the strange, beautiful statues, and tried to make herself join them.

At last she screwed up her courage to step down into the cave. She looked fearfully at the woman on whose shoulder Kiki had flown. Yes – Jack was right. She was nothing but a beautiful statue, with a finely-moulded face and a cloud of dark hair. She had magnificent jewels for eyes, and her glittering teeth were exquisite jewels too. Round her neck were golden chains, set with precious stones, and her waxen fingers gleamed with rings. Round her waist was the most beautiful belt that Lucy-Ann had ever seen, carved and set with shining red and blue stones.

There were dozens of these statues in the cave, some of men and some of women. Some of them carried small babies in their arms, fat, smiling babies dressed in the most exquisite clothes, set with thousands of tiny pearls.

It was the babies that gave Jack the clue to what the statues were.

'Do you know what they are?' he said. 'They are statues taken from churches somewhere in this country. This one represents Mary, the mother of Jesus – and the little baby is meant to be Jesus Himself. That's why they are adorned with such lovely jewels. People have spent heaps of money on them to make them beautiful.'

'Oh yes – and some of them are carried in processions at church festivals,' said Dinah, remembering how her mother had once described such a festival to her. 'Well, fancy – statues taken from churches! Whatever for?'

'Stolen, I should think,' said Jack. 'Stolen by people who took advantage of the troubled war-times, and hid them here – meaning to collect them when they had a chance.'

'They must be worth a lot of money,' said Philip, fingering the magnificent jewels. 'Gosh, I did get a terrible fright when I first saw them! I honestly thought they were real people.'

'So did I,' said Lucy-Ann, who had now recovered. 'I couldn't bear them to stand so still and silent. I nearly screamed with fright!'

'We were idiots not to guess they were statues,' said Dinah. 'I say – where does the light come from that lights these statues? It's only a faint sort of light, but it's enough to see them by quite well.'

Jack looked all round. 'It must be a sort of phosphorescent glow from the walls and roof of the cave,' he said. 'It's rather a greenish light, isn't it?'

'I say – there's another archway here!' called Philip, from beyond the statues. 'Come and see. I believe there's another cave beyond.'

They all went to see. Through the archway was yet

another cave, lighted with the same dim, greenish glow. In it were stacked great square, oblong or round, flat things. There were no statues at all. The children went to see what the flat things were.

'Pictures!' said Jack, as he tried to swing one to face him. 'Enormous ones! Where did they come from? Churches too, do you think?'

'Oh – picture galleries very likely,' said Philip. 'Maybe they are famous and quite priceless pictures – very old too. Look at that one – it looks terribly old-fashioned. My word – these things may be worth a fortune – heaps of fortunes! I remember reading not so long ago about pictures that were worth two or three million pounds!'

'I didn't know there was so much money in the world,' said Lucy-Ann, startled. She gazed in awe at the dusty, dim old pictures, tracing their great carved frames with her finger.

'Some of the pictures have been taken out of their frames to bring them here,' said Jack, pulling at a roll of thick canvas. 'Look, this one must have been cut from its frame and rolled up so as to be taken away easily.'

There were about fifty rolls of canvas besides the framed pictures. Jack shone his torch on to many of the pictures, but none of the children thought the subjects interesting. So many were portraits of rather fat and stern-looking men. Others were scenes from the Bible, or from old legends.

'Well, this really is a find!' said Jack. 'I bet if those

men could have found these, they would have made a simply enormous fortune selling them.'

'Of course – they were after all these,' said Philip. 'And that's what those crates were for. To pack them in. They meant to crate them carefully and fly them away little by little. What a brain wave on their part!'

'And Otto fooled them!' said Jack. 'Took them to a rock-fall and said the treasure cave was behind it – so they meekly gave up and flew off. What idiots!'

'And *we* found everything!' rejoiced Lucy-Ann. 'Oh, I wish we could tell Bill!'

'Are there any more caves?' wondered Jack, and walked over to the end of the second cave. 'Yes! Here's another archway and another cave. Books here! And old documents! Come and look!'

'Old books are sometimes as precious and as rare as old pictures,' said Philip, gazing round at the piles of enormous, heavily-bound books. 'I say – look at this one! It's a bible, but in a foreign language. Isn't it enormous? Look at the old printing!'

'These really *are* caves of treasure,' said Jack. 'Treasure from churches, libraries and picture galleries. I suppose the war-lords must have hidden them away, meaning to get them when peace came and make a lot of money out of their loot. How awful to steal things like this, though!'

'There's a little cave here, just off this book cave,' called Dinah, who was exploring by herself. 'There is a big chest here. Oh, and another – and another! What's in them, I wonder?'

Jack came over to her and lifted up the heavy lid of one chest. He stared down in surprise at the glittering coins piled together in the chest.

'Gold!' he said. 'The gold coinage of some country, I can't tell which. I've never seen gold coins like these before. My goodness, there's a fortune in that box too – and in that chest, and that one! Fortunes everywhere!'

'It's like a dream,' said Lucy-Ann, and she sat down on one of the chests. 'It really is. A cave of gleaming icicles, or stalags— whatever you call them! A cave of stars! A cave of glittering, jewelled statues! A cave of pictures, and a cave of old books! And now a cave of gold! I can't believe it.'

It did seem extraordinary. They all sat down on the oak chests and rested. The dim greenish light still shone everywhere, a kind of pale glow that did not seem to come from anywhere in particular, and yet was everywhere.

It was very quiet there. The children could hear themselves breathing, and a cough from Jack sounded startlingly loud.

Then another sound came through the stillness – a sound so completely unexpected and surprising that nobody could believe their ears!

'Cluck! Cluck-luck-luck!'

'Whatever's that?' said Lucy-Ann at last. 'It sounded like a hen clucking.'

'Must have been old Kiki,' said Jack, looking around for her. But she was just near by, sitting on another chest, humped up, looking rather dismal. She had had enough of caves. The children stared at her. Could it have been Kiki?

They listened to see if she would make the same noise again. But she didn't stir. And then the noise came once more, quite clearly, from another direction altogether.

'Cluck-luck-lurrrrrk! Cluck-luck-lurrrrk!'

'It *is* a hen!' said Jack, jumping up. 'Making an egg-laying noise. But – a hen – in these caves! It's impossible!'

All the children were now on their feet. Dinah pointed to some steps at the back of the little cave of gold. 'That's where the noise comes from,' she said.

'I'll go up first and see if it really *is* a hen,' said Jack. 'I can't believe it.'

He went cautiously up the steps, and at the same time the clucking began again. Kiki woke up and heard it in astonishment. She immediately began to cluck too, which evidently astonished the hidden clucker, who got very excited and let off a perfect volley of clucks.

Jack came to the top of the steps. There was another door there, but not a very stout one. It was ajar. He pushed it open a little more, very slowly, so that he might see in without attracting attention, though he did not expect to see anything but a hen.

What he saw transfixed him with astonishment. Philip dug his fingers into his back.

'Go on, Jack – what's up?'

Jack turned round to the others. 'I say,' he said in a half whisper, 'it's awfully odd – but there's a little cell-like room up here – furnished – table and chairs and a lighted lamp! And – there's a meal on the table!'

'Come down quickly then,' whispered Dinah. 'We don't want to bump into anyone. It must be someone who's guarding the treasure till the others come to get it. Come down!'

But it was too late. A curious, quavering voice came from the cell-like room into which Jack had peeped. A few strange words reached them – but they couldn't understand a single one. *Now* what was going to happen?

23

The guardians of the treasure

The children stood absolutely still, holding their breath. Who was there, in that little room at the top of the steps? The voice came again, repeating the words that the children could not understand.

Then to the top of the little flight of steps came a brown hen! It stood there, its head on one side, peering down at the children. 'Cluck!' it said, in a friendly kind of voice. 'Cluck-luck!'

'Cluck!' said Kiki at once.

Lucy-Ann clutched Dinah. 'Was it the hen talking before?' she whispered in amazement.

It wasn't, of course. The quavering voice came again, and to the children's surprise it sounded really frightened.

Nobody came to where Jack stood almost at the top of the steps. The boy screwed up his courage and marched into the little room.

At the other end of it, under a small archway or rock,

stood an old, old man. Behind him was a woman, just as old, but more bent. They stared at Jack in amazement, and then, turning to one another, they poured out a stream of hurried words that the children could not understand at all.

Lucy-Ann wondered what Jack was doing up in the little room. Somebody ought to be with him. She went up the steps and joined Jack. The two old people stared at the red-haired freckled child, so like Jack.

Then the old woman made a crooning noise, pushed past her husband and went over to Lucy-Ann. She put her arms round her and kissed her. Then she patted her hair. Lucy-Ann was surprised and not very pleased. Who was this funny old woman who suddenly seemed so affectionate?

She called to the others. 'Dinah! Philip! Come along up! It's two old people here with their hen!'

Soon all four children were in the little underground room. As soon as the old man heard them talking, he joined in eagerly, speaking English in a strange, clipped way.

'Ah, ah! You are English children! That is goot, very goot. Once, long time ago, I was in your so beautiful country. I was in a big London hotel.'

'Thank goodness he speaks English,' said Philip. 'I say – what are they doing here, with the treasure? Are they in league with the other men?'

'Have to find out,' said Jack. 'They seem quite harmless, anyhow. But there may be others.' He turned to the old man. The old woman was still making a fuss of Lucy-Ann. Evidently they had not set eyes on children for a long time.

'Who else is here besides you?' demanded Jack.

'Just me and Elsa, my old wife, and our hen Martha,' answered the old man. 'We guard all those things in the caves, till the day when they go back to their right homes. May that day come soon!'

'I don't believe the poor old things know that the war was over long ago,' said Jack to the others, in a low voice. 'I wonder who left them here to guard these things.' He turned to the old man again. 'Who told you to guard these things?' he asked.

'Julius Muller,' said the old man promptly. 'Ah, what a great man! How he worked against the enemy, even when they were shooting and bombing and burning in our valley! It was he who discovered that the enemy was using our mountain caves to hide away these treasures – treasures stolen from our churches and many other places.'

'Just what we thought,' said Philip, intensely interested. 'Go on – tell us more.'

'Then the people fled from our valley,' said the old man. 'Many were killed. The valley was empty, all save me and Elsa, my old wife. We hid with our hens and our pig, and no one found us. Then one day Julius Muller found us and ordered us to come here, by a way he knew, and guard the treasure – not for the enemy, no – but for him and the people! He said that one day the enemy would be defeated and would flee away – and then he and the others would come back to find the treasure – but he has not come.'

'He can't,' said Jack. 'The pass is blocked. No one can get in or out of this valley now – except by aeroplane. The war has been over a long time. But bad people are after the treasure – people who have heard it is hidden here, and have come to steal it.'

The old fellow looked scared and bewildered, as if he only half understood what Jack was telling him. The children thought that he must have lived so long underground that his mind could not take in much news from the outer world. To him, his wife, the treasure, and perhaps his hen, were the only things that mattered.

'Do you live here, in this room?' asked Lucy-Ann. 'Where do you get your food from? Does your hen like living underground?'

'There are great stores of food here,' said the old man. 'There is even corn for Martha, the hen. When we first came here, we had six hens and our pig. But the pig died. And one by one the hens died. Only Martha is left. She does not lay many eggs now. Perhaps one in fourteen days.'

'Cluck,' said Martha in a proud voice. She was evidently proud of her one egg a fortnight.

Kiki repeated the cluck and then went off into a series

of quacks. The hen looked surprised and alarmed. So did the two old people.

'Shut up, Kiki,' said Jack. 'You're showing off.'

'What is that bird?' asked the old man. 'Is it a – how do you call it? – a parrot?'

'Yes,' said Jack. 'She's mine. Always goes with me everywhere. But I say – don't you want to know how *we* came here?'

'Ah, yes, of course!' said the old man. 'It is all so surprising, you understand – and my wits are dull now – I cannot take in many things at once. You must tell me about yourselves, please. Wife, what about some food for these children?'

Elsa did not understand and the old man repeated what he said in her own language. She nodded and smiled a kind toothless smile. Taking Lucy-Ann by the hand, she went over to where tins and jars stood on a rocky ledge.

'She's very keen on Lucy-Ann,' said Philip. 'She can't fuss over her enough.'

The old man heard and understood. 'We had a little granddaughter,' he said. 'So like this little girl, with red hair and a sweet face. She lived with us. And one day the enemy came and took her away and we never saw her again. So now my wife sees her little lost one in your sister. You must excuse her, for maybe she really thinks her small Greta has come back.'

'Poor old things!' said Dinah. 'What an awful life

they must have led – lost under this mountain, guarding a treasure for Julius Muller, waiting for him for ages, not knowing what had happened outside in the world! If we hadn't come, they might never have come out again!'

To the children's delight, Elsa got them a really fine meal. She would not let poor Lucy-Ann leave her side, though, so the little girl had to trot everywhere with her. Jack told the old man a little of their own story, though it was plain that the old fellow did not really follow it all. His wits were dull, as he said, and he could not really understand all this sudden news from a world he had almost forgotten.

Kiki enjoyed herself enormously. Martha, the hen, was obviously used to keeping the old couple company and pecked about under the table, brushing against everyone's legs. Kiki climbed down to join her, and kept up an interested, if one-sided conversation with her.

'How many times have I told you to wipe your feet?' she asked Martha. 'Blow your nose. Put the kettle on.'

'Cluck,' answered Martha politely.

'Humpy dumpy,' went on Kiki, evidently anxious to teach Martha a few nursery rhymes now. 'See how they run! Quack, quack, quack, quack!'

The hen looked surprised, ruffled up her feathers and stared at Kiki. 'Cluck, luck, luck,' she said, and pecked up a few crumbs.

Lucy-Ann and the others giggled at this conversation. Then Lizzie also thought she would join the company, as there was plenty of food going. She ran down Philip's sleeve and appeared on the table, much to the old woman's alarm.

'Meet Dizzy Lizzie,' said Philip politely.

'I say – they must think we're queer visitors!' said Dinah, keeping a watchful eye on Lizzie in case she came any nearer. 'Walking in like this – with a parrot and a lizard – and staying to dinner!'

'I don't think they are bothering much,' said Philip. 'Just enjoying the change. It must be nice to have company after being alone so long.'

When they had finished the meal, the old woman spoke to her husband. He turned to the children.

'My wife says, are you tired? Would you like a rest? We have a beautiful place to rest in, when we want to enjoy the sun.'

This surprised the children very much. The sun! How did these old people ever see the sun – unless they went through all the cave and passages to the hole that gave on to the mountainside?

'Where do you go to rest then?' asked Jack.

'Come,' said the old man, and led him out of the little cell-like room. Elsa took Lucy-Ann by the hand. They all followed the old man. He went along a broad passage, hollowed out of the rock.

'I should think most of these tunnels were hollowed out by underground rivers at some time or other,' said Jack. 'Then they took a different course, and the tunnels dried up, and became these passages, linking all the caves together.'

The passage twisted a little and then quite suddenly came into daylight. The children found themselves on a flat ledge of rock, hung about by ferns and other plants, full in the sun. How simply delicious!

'Another way into the treasure caves,' said Dinah. But she was wrong. Nobody could possibly enter the caves by way of the ledge. The ledge of rock jutted over a great precipice that fell sheer down many hundreds of feet. No one, not even a goat, could climb up or down to it. It was, as the old man said, a fine, sunny resting place – but that was all.

Martha pecked about on the ledge of rock, though what she could find there the children couldn't imagine. Kiki sat near by and watched her. She had formed a firm friendship with Martha. The children rather liked Martha themselves. She was such a nice, plump little thing, friendly and natural, and as much of a pet to the old couple as Kiki was to them.

They all lay down in the sun. It was delicious to feel its warm rays after being so long underground. As they lay there they heard something rumbling in the distance.

'The waterfall,' said Lucy-Ann. 'Fancy – we must be fairly near it, if we can hear it!'

They lay there sleepily. The old fellow sat on a rock near by, smoking a pipe. He seemed very contented. Elsa had disappeared.

'Isn't it strange to think we've found the treasure – and can't do anything about it at all!' said Dinah. 'We're stuck here. No way of getting word to anyone. And never will have, as far as I can see, till the pass into the valley is unblocked – and that may not be for ages!'

'Oh dear – don't say such gloomy things,' begged Lucy-Ann. 'Anyway, the men are gone. That's one good thing. I felt awfully afraid when they were in the valley too. Thank goodness they've gone!'

She spoke too soon. There came a familiar throbbing noise – and the children sat up at once.

'The plane's back! Blow! Those men will be about again now – and maybe they've even got the real truth out of Otto – where the treasure *really* is!' said Jack. 'We shall have to be jolly careful now.'

24

Juan finds the caves

The children held a council of war. What would be the best thing to do? Suppose the men did know the way into the treasure caves now, and came to them? They would begin to take away the treasure, that was certain.

'And we can't stop them,' said Philip. 'They are jolly tough men. They wouldn't let a pack of children and two old people prevent them from taking what they wanted. I can't think why they've come back unless it is to search for the treasure again and find it this time.'

Everyone agreed with Jack. 'If only we could escape and get news to Bill,' sighed Philip. 'But there simply isn't a way.'

The plane had not come into sight – they had only heard the sound of its engines. The old man did not seem to have heard anything at all. The children decided not to tell him, in case he got into a panic.

'What do you think it would be best for us to do?' said Philip. 'Stay here with the old couple and see if the men do come and take anything away? We can hide somewhere quite easily. Or go back to our own fern cave beyond the waterfall? I always felt safe there. And we've got plenty of food there too.'

'There's plenty here,' said Dinah. 'Let's stay here. After all, if the men do come, we can hide in that stalactite cave – there are plenty of hiding places there, behind those frozen columns. They won't see us. One of us could always be on guard there, to see who comes in or out.'

'Perhaps you're right,' said Jack. 'We must just wait and see what happens. Once the men really do find the treasure caves, there will be a lot of coming and going – taking the treasure to the plane – taking off with it in the air – coming back again to fetch more – and so on.'

'Shouldn't be surprised if they bring more planes here, as soon as they've discovered exactly where the treasure is,' said Philip. 'It would be a slow business taking one or two crates at a time.'

'Lucy-Ann is asleep,' said Dinah. 'I think I'll snooze too. It's so lovely here in the sun. Those men won't be along yet, so nobody needs to be on guard in the caves.'

'It would be almost better to be on guard at the entrance,' said Philip thoughtfully. 'Then we could spot anyone in plenty of time.'

'Yes, that's a much better idea,' said Jack, settling down to snooze too. 'I'm sure the men won't be along today. The sun's going down. They'll wait till tomorrow.'

That night the children spent in the old couple's 'bedroom.' It was a smallish cave leading off from their 'sitting room,' where the children had had their meal. In the 'bedroom' was a pile of rugs, spotlessly clean, and the old people insisted on giving up this room to the children.

'We can sleep in chairs,' said the old man. 'That will be no hardship.'

The old woman covered Lucy-Ann up carefully and even kissed her goodnight. 'She really thinks I'm Greta, her lost grandchild,' said Lucy-Ann. 'I just can't stop her making a fuss of me, because I'm so sorry for her.'

In the morning, after another good meal, Jack said he was going to take first watch at the entrance to the passage that led to the caves. Philip was to take second watch, two hours later.

The boy settled himself down on the edge of the hole, under the big slab of rock that stuck out from the hillside. It was a fine sunny morning. The others thought they would go and examine some of the statues in the statue cave, and the old man said he would tell them their histories, and where they had come from.

Jack sat there, gazing out down the hillside. He could see a long way. He could see scores of high mountains around, one behind the other. The pine forests on them looked like short grass. He put his field glasses to his eyes to watch the birds around.

It was a disappointing district for wild birds. There

seemed to be very few. Jack swung his glasses from side to side of the hill, examining everything.

And then he suddenly got a tremendous shock. He had trained his glasses on to a bush, behind which he thought he had seen a quick movement. He had wondered if some bird or animal was hiding there.

He saw no bird. Instead, he saw the head and shoulders of Juan – and Juan was gazing steadily up at him through a pair of field glasses, just as Jack was gazing down at him through field glasses too!

Jack was simply petrified. He stared down through his glasses, and Juan stared up, each seeing the other quite clearly. So Juan had come once more to seek the treasure! Had he come to that cliff-side by chance – or had he got the same map from Otto that Jack had had?

'I've given the show away properly now,' thought Jack angrily. 'I've only got to pop into this hole and he'll know where the entrance is at once. But if I wander away on the hillside, he'll be after me. What a fix I'm in!'

Juan did not take his eyes off Jack. He knelt there by the bush, his field glasses fixed on the boy, watching his every movement.

'He can't possibly see the hole that I'm sitting on the edge of,' thought Jack. 'I think perhaps it would be best if I left this place and began to climb up the hillside. If I do, and Juan follows, he may miss the hole altogether.'

He was about to do this, when Philip leapt up beside him.

'My turn now, Freckles,' said Philip. 'Hallo, what are you looking at?'

'Pity you came just then,' said Jack. 'There is Juan down there, Philip – and he's got his glasses trained on to me – and on you too now! I was just about to crawl up the hillside to make him chase me, and perhaps miss this hole, when you came. Now he'll know there's a cave here and he'll be up in no time.'

'Golly!' said Philip, alarmed. 'We'd better warn the others at once then.'

'Yes, it's the only thing to do now,' said Jack, and he jumped back into the hole. 'Come on. It won't take Juan long to be up here. Blow! Why didn't I think he might be about already?'

They made their way quickly along the passage and through the many caves. They came to the little cell-like room and found the others there. Jack hurriedly told them what had happened.

'We must hide,' he said. But the old couple did not seem to take this in. They would not hide.

'We have nothing to be afraid of,' said the old man in a dignified manner. 'They will not hurt us.'

'You have plenty to be afraid of,' said Jack desperately. 'Do come and hide!'

But they wouldn't. Jack could not waste any more time in arguing, because he wanted to get the girls to safety. He hurried them off.

'In the cave of stalactites?' asked Dinah. Jack nodded.

But when he came to the cave of silent statues, he paused. Wouldn't this be a better place? Suppose they all stood at the back, in the dim shadows, and posed like statues? Would anyone notice them? It was worth trying.

'Take shawls off some of the figures,' said the boy. 'Wrap them round you. Stand quite still right at the back there.'

It didn't take long to drape themselves and stand right at the back. 'Do you remember that game called statues that we used to play?' whispered Lucy-Ann. 'You had to stand quite still, or you were caught. I feel like that now.'

'Well, be sure you stand still or you *will* be caught,' said Jack. 'Sh! Isn't that somebody?'

'Shhhhhh!' said Kiki at once. Jack smacked her on her beak.

'Be quiet! Do you want to give us away, silly bird?'

Kiki opened her beak to squawk and then thought better of it. She flew off somewhere and disappeared. Jack was quite glad to see her go, for he didn't want her chattering and attracting attention to them.

A noise came from the tunnel beyond. Somebody was already there. It must be Juan.

'He's already gone through the cave of stalactites and the cave of stars,' whispered Philip. 'Now he's in the tunnel leading here. He'll be at the door in a minute. Pity we didn't shut it. He might not have guessed how to twist that iron stud to get it open.'

The door was almost closed, but not shut. As the

children watched it, in the dim greenish glow of the cave, they saw it slowly pushed open. Then the gleaming barrel of a revolver came round it. Juan was evidently taking no chances.

Lucy-Ann gulped. Oh dear! She hoped the gun wouldn't go off. She didn't like guns at all.

The door was opened wide and Juan stood there, revolver in hand. He gasped when he saw the silent figures standing about, their curious eyes gleaming.

'Put your hands up!' said Juan sharply, to the statues. The statues did nothing of the sort. Juan's hand trembled. The children guessed he was feeling panicky as they had felt when they too had first seen the strange silent company.

'Wipe your feet!' ordered a sharp voice, and the children jumped violently. It was Kiki. She was sitting just above Juan, on a ledge of rock.

'Who's there?' shouted Juan. 'I tell you I'll shoot if anyone moves.'

The statues didn't move – not even the four live ones.

'Who's there?' called Juan again.

'Three blind mice,' answered Kiki, and went off into a terrible cackle of laughter. It was almost too much for Juan. He backed a little, and tried to see which of the statues was talking.

'Pop goes the weasel!' said Kiki, and then began to cluck like Martha. Juan's hand trembled again. But he advanced a little, going down the step into the cave.

Then he saw, as the children had seen, that the figures were only bejewelled statues, and he laughed loudly.

'Fool!' he said to himself.

'Fool!' repeated Kiki, and Juan swung round at once.

'Who's there? One of you children, I suppose. Wait till I get you!'

Kiki began to mew like a cat. The man looked for this unexpected cat, then decided it was one of the children again, playing a trick on him. Kiki flew silently to the next cave and began to talk to herself there.

'One, two, button my shoe, see how they run!'

The man took one more glance at the company of statues and went into the next cave. The children heaved a sigh of relief. But they dared not move yet.

It seemed a very long time till the man came back. With him came the two old people, evidently very frightened. Juan shouted at them in their own language, and the children could not understand a word.

Then, without another glance at the statues, Juan went through the stout oaken door and shut it. The bang echoed loudly through the cave and made everyone jump.

Then they heard another sound which made their hearts sink. It was the noise of strong bolts being shot home on the other side of the door.

Crash! Crash, crash! All three bolts were shot firmly into place. Now the door could not possibly be opened from the inside.

'Did you hear that?' groaned Jack. 'We're prisoners now. If only we'd hidden in the cave of stalactites or the cave of stars, we'd have been all right. We could have got out of the hole. Now we can't. We'll have to stay here till the men set us free – if they ever do.'

25

Philip's astonishing plan

The old couple looked panic-stricken when four of the statues apparently talked and came alive. But when the children took off their borrowed draperies and carefully gave them back to the right statues again, the old couple saw who they were.

Elsa came running to Lucy-Ann and hugged her. The old man stood trembling.

'What did he say to you?' demanded Jack.

'He said he was going to make us prisoners here, and that he was bringing others back with him to remove all our treasure,' said the old man. Tears suddenly poured down his cheeks. 'He is a bad man. Have I guarded these beautiful things all this time to let them fall into the hands of a man so bad?'

'It's sickening,' said Jack. 'We simply can't do a thing! We shall just have to stand by and watch those rogues take away everything, pack them into crates and fly off with them!'

'Let's go out to that sunny ledge,' said Dinah. 'I can't bear this gloom any more. I shall feel better when we are out there. Let's ask the old man if his wife would bring a picnic meal out there, Jack. You and Philip can help her to bring it. I can't think properly down here in the dark, with all those statues trying to listen.'

'All right,' said Jack, seeing that Dinah was on the point of tears. 'You go off with Lucy-Ann and Kiki. We'll soon come. You'll feel better in the sunshine.'

'Wasn't Kiki clever to lead the man away from us?' said Lucy-Ann. 'He *was* scared when she suddenly spoke to him. So should I have been! I should have thought it was one of the statues speaking.'

She and Dinah made their way to the sunny ledge. Dinah threw herself down there thankfully.

'I don't like this adventure any more, Dinah, do you?' asked Lucy-Ann. 'It's not so bad if there's something we can *do* – but we seem to be helpless here.'

'I like to make adventures go the way I want them to,' said Dinah rather sulkily. 'I don't like them to make me do things I don't like. Don't talk to me, Lucy-Ann. I shall snap at you. I feel cross.'

'It's only because of the strain we went through whilst we were pretending to be statues,' said Lucy-Ann.

'Don't sound so grown-up,' snapped Dinah. 'It's not that – I just feel bad tempered because I want to get out of this valley and I can't.'

Lucy-Ann said nothing more. She settled down in the

sun, waiting for the picnic that Jack and Philip would soon be bringing out with Elsa. Kiki sat murmuring to herself near by. Martha the hen arrived and began pecking about companionably. Kiki talked to her, and she clucked back.

Dinah forgot her bad temper when the others came out with a picnic meal. They had a good feast and then discussed all the morning's happening once more. In the middle of the discussion they heard the sound of the plane again, and this time saw it rising high into the sky.

'Why, they're off again!' said Jack in surprise. 'Why?'

'Probably to get other men along to help in removing everything, now they really do know where the treasure is,' said Philip. 'And as you suggested, Jack – they might even bring more planes.'

It was hateful feeling that they were complete prisoners. Jack and Philip went desperately to the bolted door once and tried to move it – but it was hopeless of course. The bolts were old but still very strong.

There was nothing to do, and they felt bored. They went to examine the statues more closely and to look at the old pictures and the musty old books.

The statues were loaded with magnificent jewels. Some of the figures were really beautifully made and dressed, but others were crude and garish. Each one, however, was adorned with jewels, though the children were not able to tell if all the gleaming brooches, dazzling earrings and necklaces, glittering bracelets, belts and rings were really valuable or not. Probably some were, and others were only semi-precious.

'I expect the men will strip the statues of their jewellery, and take only that, leaving the figures behind,' said Jack. 'They will crate the pictures and books.'

'Why couldn't we strip the jewels off and hide them away somewhere so that the men wouldn't get them?' suddenly said Dinah. 'I don't see why wicked men like that should have them.'

'Good idea!' said Jack. 'Come on – we'll take the jewellery now and hide it somewhere!'

But as soon as they began to remove it, the old couple flew at them in horror.

'Not do that! Ah, bad boy!' cried the old man, removing a brooch from Jack's hand.

'We only want to hide the things from those men,' protested Jack. 'They'll be back and steal these things soon.'

'They belong to these,' said the old man, waving his hand towards the statues. 'They must not be removed by anyone. It is against the law of the Church.'

The children did not try again. It was plain that Elsa and the old man would fly into a rage if they attempted to. They seemed to think that it was a very wicked and unholy act to take away any of the adornments belonging to the figures.

The long day passed at last. Nobody slept very well that night. They were worried about what was going to happen. It was horrid to feel they were at the mercy of rogues like Juan.

They were all out on the sunny ledge the next morning, early, having breakfast there. They had no meals in the caves now if they could help it.

'Listen,' said Dinah suddenly. 'I can hear the plane coming back.'

They all listened, the old couple too. The noise grew louder. It became very loud indeed. Then Jack leapt to his feet.

'It's not just one plane! It's many! Look, there's one! – circling down – and another over there! – and here comes another! Gracious! Juan's got quite a fleet of planes!'

There were four altogether. Evidently Juan meant to do the job properly. The children pictured the planes landing one by one on the long wide strip of grass at the bottom of the valley.

'Now we can expect things to happen,' said Jack. 'The whole of the treasure will be gone soon.'

'What a shame!' said Dinah. 'And we can't do a thing to stop it!'

'If *only* we could get word to Bill!' said Jack desperately. 'But there's no way out of the valley except in one of those planes.'

Philip stared at Jack a moment. Then he said something so exciting that the others could hardly believe their ears.

'Yes – that's the only way out. And I'm going to take it.'

There was silence. Then Jack spoke, astonished.

'Whatever do you mean? You can't fly a plane.'

'Of course not. But I can *hide* in one!' said Philip. 'Didn't we hide, all of us, in a plane, coming here? Well, why shouldn't I hide in one *leaving* here? I bet I could hide unseen – and slip out when I had a chance, and get word to Bill about everything.'

'Philip! It's a *grand* idea!' said Jack. 'But I'll go, not you.'

'You jolly well won't!' said Philip. 'It's *my* idea! Nobody else is going to pinch such a gorgeous idea. I'm going, see?'

'I don't want either of you to go,' said Lucy-Ann. 'You might be seen. Something awful might happen to you. Don't leave us.'

'Jack will be with you,' said Philip. 'And the old couple. You'll be all right. I tell you, it's the only way to get help – to fly off in one of the planes, when the men go on their next trip. They'll have to come back two or three times to take all these things – and, if only I can get word to Bill, he can catch the men actually doing the stealing!'

'It sounds too good to be true,' said Dinah. 'I don't believe you can do it. Anyway – how are you even going to get to the plane? You know we're bolted in. Nobody can get out.'

'I shall watch my chance and slip out through that

door when the men are going to and fro,' said Philip, enjoying his planning. 'Then I shall hide in the cave of stalactites and go up the passage to the hole as soon as I can. Then I'll get along back to the planes, and choose one to hop into. I don't reckon they will have left anyone on guard there, as they think we're all well and truly imprisoned.'

'It sounds easy, but it won't be,' said Jack. 'Better let me do it, Tufty.'

'Think again!' said Philip. 'This is my own pet adventure, see?'

'You might even be able to squeeze into a crate,' said Dinah thoughtfully. 'Nobody would think of looking into a packed crate.'

'Good idea!' said Philip. 'In fact, jolly good!'

'Well, we can expect quite a horde of men here today,' said Jack. 'It will surprise the poor old couple. They will be in a dreadful state when they see their well-guarded treasure going.'

'Philip, we won't pretend that we are any of the statues today when the men come,' said Dinah. 'Only you. The men are sure to have a hunt round for us if they can't find us today, so we'd better all be found, except you. You can be a statue again, and wait your chance to rush out of the door.'

'Yes. I think I will,' said Philip. 'It may not work, but it's the only thing to do. Now – when will those men be along? It will take them about an hour and a half to get here. It's half an hour since we saw the planes. I mustn't leave it to the last minute to put myself in place.'

'Better go now,' said Lucy-Ann, who was on pins and needles about the whole thing. 'We'll come with you and see that you're in a good place and really look like a statue.'

They all went down the passage, and made their way through the various caves to the one in which the statues stood. Martha the hen came too. She had attached herself to Jack now, and followed him wherever he went. She had laid an egg that morning, and the old woman had made Lucy-Ann have it for breakfast.

'Look! – there's a half-hidden ledge here not far from the door,' said Dinah eagerly. 'If you stood there you would hardly be seen, it's so dark there. And you would be near the door to creep out if you got a chance.'

'Yes, that does seem the best place,' said Philip. 'It really does. Now what about a shawl or something to drape over my head? I don't want my short hair to give me away.'

They found a very big shawl and draped it carefully round him. He went to stand on the little ledge, and everyone agreed that it was a splendid place.

'You can hardly be seen,' said Jack. 'Well, good luck, Tufty. We'll go now, and we shan't hide. We shall let the men see us and hope they'll think there's nobody else in the caves at all. If you can't escape we shall know, because you'll still be about tonight.'

'Goodbye,' said Philip, looking exactly like a statue. 'Don't worry about me. I'll be off and away soon, and I'll get word to Bill and Mother. We'll soon rescue you, don't you worry!'

26

The getaway

In about an hour's time Philip heard the sound of foot-steps and then the bolts of the door were shot back. Juan's revolver appeared round the opening door again. But this time there was no Kiki to talk to him – nobody to be seen or heard except the silent company of statues.

Juan came down into the cave. Other men followed him. Philip watched them through a fold of the shawl. He hoped they wouldn't start stripping the jewels off the statues at once, or they might discover him.

The men exclaimed in wonder at the statues. They had powerful torches with them which they switched on at once. Philip was not prepared for that. He shrank back into his corner, glad of the draping shawl.

The men were a rough-looking lot, and they called out to one another in surprise as they saw the gleaming jewels on the necks and arms of the statues. Some of them grabbed brooches and necklaces at once. Juan gave a sharp order and the men replaced them sulkily.

Philip counted the men. There were eight. Otto was not among them, but that was not surprising. Juan, Pepi and Luis were there. There were two men for each aeroplane, apparently.

Juan led the way to the next cave, through the tunnel. Their footsteps echoed hollowly as they passed through. Philip wondered if they would all go on to the next cave – and the next. If so, he could slip out of the open door straight away, and make his way down the hillside at once.

He listened. He could hear the men's voices from the next cave, where the pictures were. Then footsteps again, farther away. Then only a faint murmur of voices.

'They've gone to the cave of books – and then they'll go to the cave where the gold is,' thought Philip. 'I've plenty of time to get through the door and away.'

He dropped his shawl on the floor and went quietly to the door. He was through it in a trice. Up the winding steps he went, off to the cave of stars – then to the cave of gleaming stalactites. He began to feel safer. He didn't think there would be anyone on guard outside the hole, but he meant to be careful there.

There was nobody on guard. The hillside was empty. Philip climbed out of the hole and began to make his way downwards. Soon he was well on his way, keeping a sharp look-out the whole time just in case all the men had not gone down into the caves.

He was tired and hungry by the time he reached the

men's hut. Thank goodness the door was open and there was nobody about! The boy got himself a good meal. He found a box containing bars of chocolate, and slipped some of the bars into his pocket, in case he had to go some time without food.

Then he went along to the planes. There they were, four of them, looking quite big as he walked beside them. Which should he get into?

He climbed up into the cabin of each and looked inside. In the last one there was a big heap of coats and rugs. It seemed the best plane to get into. He could pile the things over him and hide himself that way. He didn't at the moment see any chance of squeezing himself into a crate, as Dinah had suggested. Anyway, the crates were not in the plane, they were under the tarpaulins, where they had always been.

Having decided exactly what he was going to do, he had plenty of time left on his hands. He knew that the men would not be back for some time. They would be carrying heavy, awkward loads and would go far more slowly than he had gone.

He amused himself by snooping around. He went into the hut and found a coat hanging up there. He ran his hands through the pockets, thinking that any information he could get hold of might be useful to Bill, when he got to him.

There was a notebook in one of the pockets. Philip flipped over the pages. He could make nothing of it. It contained sentences in some kind of code, and plenty of numbers. Perhaps Bill could make head or tail of it. He couldn't!

He went to the cowshed. There was nothing to be seen there but the still-open tins of fruit, swarming with flies. Philip stared at them. 'Oh yes – they are what Jack left for Otto,' he thought. 'Ugh, look at the flies!'

He took a stick, dug a hole and buried the evil-smelling tins and their contents. Then he strolled off again and came to the tree where they had all once hidden. He squinted up and saw something. 'Golly, what's that?'

Then he remembered. 'Of course – we left our suitcases up there. I'd forgotten all about them. Fancy them still being there!'

He debated whether to get them down and hide them. 'No,' he thought, 'they might be found, and then the men might start looking for me. I'll leave them there.'

He kept a good look out for the returning men as the afternoon wore on. He helped himself to some biscuits and a tin of peaches at about five o'clock. Still no sign of the men.

But about ten minutes later he saw them far away in the distance. He was by the planes, waiting, ready to jump into the one he had chosen as soon as he saw the men coming.

He counted the men quickly. Yes – eight – so they

were all back. He climbed up the steps and leapt into the cabin. He went to the pile of rugs and coats and got underneath, pulling them over him so that not even the toe of his shoe showed.

'Good thing it's a hot day,' he thought. 'The men certainly won't want their coats or macks.'

He heard the voices of the men. Evidently they were pleased with their successful day. Then there was a silence. They had passed the planes, and were on their way to the hut. 'Probably get themselves a meal, and then pack up the things they have brought from the treasure caves,' thought Philip. He yawned. He felt sleepy now that he was lying down.

Soon he was asleep, and he slept so soundly that he did not even stir when, some hours later, two men entered his plane. But he did wake when the propellers swung round as the engines suddenly roared out! He nearly gave himself away by sitting up in a fright.

Then he remembered where he was, and lay perfectly still, wondering if it was nighttime. He could see nothing under the pile of coats, of course. It might have been midnight or noon for all he knew.

One by one the planes took off. Philip's plane went last of all. He felt it leave the ground like a bird and then he was away in the air.

'They haven't seen me! They don't guess they've got me on board!' thought Philip, delighted. 'It was easy after all. Hurrah!'

He fell asleep again, and the planes roared on through the night. Where were they going? To a secret landing-place? To an ordinary aerodrome?

The other children, who were sleeping that night out on the ledge, heard the roar of the planes as they left. It was such a hot night that they had felt stifled indoors and had begged the old couple to let them take the rugs out on the ledge.

'You will not walk in your sleep?' the old man had said. 'You might walk off the ledge!'

'Not one of us walks in our sleep,' said Jack. 'We'll be all right.'

Elsa, the old woman, had not wanted Lucy-Ann to sleep out on the ledge at all, and had almost cried when Lucy-Ann had insisted. Kiki and Martha were both there too. But the lizard wasn't. She was with Philip, sharing his adventure.

The children had had a horrid day. The men had found both them and the old couple in the 'sitting room' and had shouted at them and questioned them, and frightened them very much. The old man had told them that he had been living in the caves for a long time, guarding the treasure, and the men had jumped to the conclusion that the children also had been living there with them.

'Good thing they didn't ask us how we got to this valley,' said Jack afterwards. 'They just took it for granted that we and the old people came here together ages ago.'

The old man and woman had rushed to the rescue of their beloved statues when the men had begun to strip off the jewellery. The men had struck the poor old things and shouted at them. The old man had taken his weeping, trembling wife away, and the children had done their best to comfort them.

They had not gone near the men again, but had gone to sit on the sunny ledge, and wondered if Philip had managed to escape. 'I'm sure he did,' said Lucy-Ann. 'All the men kept together, and Philip could easily have slipped out of the cave of statues when they came to question us.'

The men had gone at last, taking with them a haul of jewels, one very precious figure, some pictures and a few old papers. Two of them carried a box of the gold between them. The children pictured their difficulties, hauling it up and down the mountainside.

The men had bolted the door behind them again, and once more the little company were prisoners. How they wondered what was happening to Philip! Had he managed to hide in one of the aeroplanes? Would he slip into a crate? When would the planes go off?

They knew that the planes had gone when they awoke in the night to hear the throb of the engines. They all sat up and listened. Kiki gave a squawk and pecked Martha to wake her.

'There go the planes,' said Jack. 'I bet Philip's in one. Now we shall soon be rescued. What a shock for Bill when he hears all about us! Do you think Bill will fly over in his aeroplane too?'

'I hope so,' said Lucy-Ann fervently. 'I'm longing to see Bill again. I sometimes feel as if we'll be in this valley all our lives.'

'Don't be silly,' said Dinah. 'Oh, Kiki, leave Martha alone. Whatever are you doing to her to make her cluck like that?'

'Shhhh!' said Kiki cheekily.

'Don't talk back to me!' said Dinah, lying down again. 'Well, I'm glad we heard those planes. Good luck to you, Philip, wherever you are!'

'Good luck!' called the others, and Kiki echoed the words too. 'Good luck!'

'Cluck-luck-luck!' said Martha the hen, sounding exactly as if she was joining in with the good wishes as well!

27

A discovery – and a fine idea

The next day the men were all back again in the four planes. They soon arrived once more at the treasure caves, going through the old books and papers, unrolling the dozens of canvases and looking at the pictures. They had gone to find the children and the old couple and had shouted at them again.

They had found out that somebody had helped himself to food from the hut, and they could not make it out. Hadn't they imprisoned all the children and the old people in the caves?

The children, of course, guessed at once that it was Philip who had helped himself to the food. But they were not going to say so. So Jack put on a bewildered air and replied quite stupidly, and Dinah did the same. Lucy-Ann sobbed and the men soon gave up questioning her.

As for the old couple, they knew nothing, of course. They did not even appear to have missed Philip. The men gave up their questioning after a while, and returned to their work.

Elsa was sad to see Lucy-Ann sobbing. She took her by the hand and led her into the 'bedroom.' She took down a picture she had put on a ledge there, and showed Lucy-Ann a space behind. Lucy-Ann stared at it.

'What is it?' she said. Then she called to Jack. 'Jack! Come here, and bring the old man. The old woman doesn't understand what I say.'

They came, and when Jack saw the yawning space behind the picture, he turned to the old man.

'What's that? A hidey-hole?'

'Oh, it is only a hole in the wall,' said the old fellow. 'My wife did not like it, so she covered it with a picture.'

The old woman poured out a torrent of words to him. He turned to Jack. 'My wife is sad because your little sister is frightened by those men. She says she can hide in this hole and they will not find her.'

'Let me see what it's like,' said Jack, and climbed into it. It was more than a hole. It was a tiny, round dark tunnel that had once been a waterway. Where could it lead to – if it led anywhere?

'It's a little tunnel!' Jack called back. 'Rather like the one that led out of our fern cave into the cave of echoes. I'll see if it goes anywhere.'

He crawled on for some way, and then it suddenly dipped down so steeply that he could have slid down it if it had not been so narrow. It ended in a hole that seemed to open out in the roof of a much bigger passage. Jack flashed his torch down. Yes, that really *was* a passage down there! He crawled back to the girls.

'Come behind me,' he said. 'I may have found a way of escape. We'll have to use a rope though.'

They crawled in single file till they came to the hole that dropped into the wide passage. Jack undid the rope he always carried round his waist. He tied it to a rock and let it drop down into the passage, then down he went.

The girls followed. Jack flashed his torch up and down the passage. 'Which way shall we go?' he said.

'I can hear a funny noise,' said Lucy-Ann. 'It's the waterfall, I do believe!'

They went down the passage towards the noise – and to their intense surprise and delight they came out on to the ledge behind the waterfall, the one on which Lucy-Ann and Dinah had capered about to hold the attention of Pepi some days before.

'I *say*! It's the waterfall ledge – and that is the passage that leads back to the cave of echoes!' said Jack. 'Would you believe it? We can get back to our old fern cave and we shan't be prisoners in the treasure caves any more. Let's go and fetch the old couple too.'

He went back down the passage, swarmed up the rope, wriggled back up the little tunnel and came out into the sitting room. He told the old man where the passage led to. 'Come too,' he said. 'We will take you to a safe place.'

The old man laughed sadly. 'We cannot do as you do and crawl and climb,' he said. 'It is impossible. You go, and we will put back the picture over the hole and no one will guess.'

Jack went back to the girls, Kiki with him. 'Pity we couldn't take Martha too,' he said. 'I got quite fond of her. But the old people would miss her. They simply won't come with us. I think they're right too – they'd never be able to swarm along that little tunnel, and swing down that rope – nor would they ever be able to get down into the fern cave. Come on! I'm longing to get back to our own cave. Ha ha – we've escaped after all! Won't those men be wild!'

'I hope they won't hurt those two old people,' said Lucy-Ann anxiously. 'She is such a dear, gentle old woman.'

They went down the winding passage and came to the cave of echoes, where Kiki annoyed them by squawking and screeching all the time, bringing back echoes of hundreds of magnified squawks and screeches that almost deafened them.

They got through the little drainpipe-like tunnel that led to the back of the fern cave, and dropped thankfully down to the rugs still spread out there.

'Home again,' said Jack, and laughed. 'Funny to think we feel this is home – but I really do.'

They settled down for a rest. 'Those men must have gone off somewhere in their planes last night, unloaded their goods and taken off again almost at once to get back so quickly,' said Dinah thoughtfully. 'I really hardly expected to see them in the caves today. I didn't hear the planes come back, did you?'

'No – but the wind has changed, so maybe the sound didn't blow in our direction,' said Jack. 'It's not so sunny now – looks like rain again. The wind's jolly strong.'

'We shall have to keep a look out for Bill and Philip if they come,' said Dinah. 'Philip won't know we're here, will he?'

'Do you girls mind if I go this evening and just have a snoop round about the men's hut?' asked Jack. 'You know – in case by any chance old Tufty didn't get away but got caught and is a prisoner.'

'Golly! I didn't even *think* of that!' said Lucy-Ann in horror. 'Oh, Jack, surely you don't think he got caught, do you?'

'Not for a minute,' said Jack cheerfully. 'But it would be just as well to make sure. I'd better go now whilst the men are busy in the caves. By the way, were all eight of them there, do you know?'

'I *think* so,' said Dinah, frowning. 'But I really couldn't be certain. Do you remember, Lucy-Ann?'

'No. I didn't look at them,' said Lucy-Ann. 'Horrid things!'

'I expect they were all there,' said Jack. 'Brr-r-r-r – the

wind's cold today. I'll put on an extra jersey. So long, girls, I'll be back in a short time!'

Off he went, following the familiar way back to the men's hut. He did not think that Philip would have been caught, but still, he must make sure. He scouted cautiously about. The hut door was shut. He went up to it and peeped in at the window. No Philip there. Good!

'Better just pop up to the cowshed,' thought Jack. 'They might have got him tied up there.' So off he went. No – it was empty – good!

There was a sudden rush of wind such as often sweeps through a mountainside valley. A torrent of rain came down and the boy ran for a tree. It was the tree in which they had once all hidden, a good big thick one, that would keep the rain off. He crouched there whilst the wind whipped round him.

There was such a noise of wind that the boy did not hear footsteps coming behind the tree. He did not see the burly figure of Pepi there, staring in surprise at the crouched boy.

In a trice Pepi was round the tree and had got hold of Jack's shoulders. The boy gave a howl of fright. Pepi gripped him tightly.

'Let me go!' yelled Jack. 'You brute, let me go! You're twisting my shoulder!'

Pepi took up a stick and grinned. 'A little of this will do you good,' he said. 'You boys are a lot of trouble to us. Where are the others? You will tell me or I will beat you black and blue.'

'Let me go!' yelled Jack, and kicked hard at Pepi's ankles. The man gave a yelp of pain and hit Jack on the back with the heavy stick. Jack kicked him again.

What would have happened to poor Jack is easy to guess – if something hadn't happened to Pepi first! The wind howled round and shook the tree violently. Something fell from the tree and hit the raging man full on the shoulder. He dropped down at once, shouting, clutching at his shoulder. Jack sped off into the wind. He turned and looked back. Pepi was trying to get up, groaning. The wind howled again, and the big tree spat out something else that hit Pepi on the head. He fell back and did not move.

'Golly!' said Jack, staring. 'It's two of our suitcases that we left up the tree! They just blew down at the right moment. I hope they haven't killed him.'

He went back cautiously to the still man. No, he wasn't killed – just completely knocked out. Jack saw his chance at once. He took his rope and roped the man's hands firmly together, and then his feet. Then he tied him to the tree.

'Now you won't be able to come after me, my dear Pepi,' said Jack, taking a quick look up the tree in case the remaining two suitcases should come down. 'I suppose the others left you here on guard today, as they knew somebody had been at the food. Well, you won't be much use as a guard for the rest of the day, but never mind. The tree will shelter you from the storm.'

Suddenly such an extraordinary idea struck Jack that he stood perfectly still and gasped. Then he struck his hands together and yelled out loudly: 'I must do it, I must, I must! But have I time? Have I time?'

He began to run as fast as he could through the wind and the rain. 'Why didn't I think of it before? If those men are in the treasure caves, I can bolt the door on them, just as they did to us – and make them prisoners! Why didn't I think of it before? It may be too late now.'

He ran and ran, gasping and panting, hot as fire in spite of the wind and the rain.

'It won't be any good. The men will be out of the caves by now,' he thought. 'I may see them at any minute. Oh, why didn't I think of this before? I could have gone and bolted them in before I left Dinah and Lucy-Ann!'

It certainly was a most wonderful idea. The men would be absolute prisoners. They did not know the way out behind the picture, and would never think of looking for it there. Certainly the old people would not tell them. Oh, if only they were still in the caves!

The rain poured down. The wind blew like a gale. Fortunately it was behind Jack now and it helped him on. He was soaked through, but he didn't care.

There was no sign of the men. Jack slowed down

when he came near the waterfall. He didn't want to run right into them. He began to think more calmly.

'Maybe they won't come out till the rain stops and the storm dies down. Rain would spoil the old books and papers and pictures. Yes, they'll be sure to wait. I may be in time yet. The men may even decide to stay the night there if the storm doesn't clear.'

Jack was right. The men, having looked out of the entrance hole of the caves, had seen the rain storm sweeping over the mountainside and had decided not to venture out with their treasures. They would be ruined.

'Better spend the night here,' said one of the men. 'In that room with the rugs. We'll turn the old people and children out.'

Only the old people were there. They made vague gestures when the men asked where the children were, pointing towards the passage that led to the sunny ledge. The men settled down on the rugs, and one of them got out a pack of cards. He set the lamp so that they could all see, and then began to deal the cards. The old people went into their 'sitting room,' sad and afraid. How they hoped that the men would not look behind the picture in the next room!

When Jack arrived at the treasure caves he could hardly walk through the passages. He stumbled along, past the cave of stalactites, past the cave of stars and into the first treasure cave, through the open door at the bottom of the curving stairway. He could see no men at all.

His heart sank. Had they gone then? Had he missed them?

He went cautiously on. When he came to the 'sitting room' he peeped in and saw the old couple there, with Martha the hen.

Then he heard the noise of the men in the next room. He beckoned to the old couple. They rose silently and followed him in surprise. Jack did not speak till he was well out of earshot of the men.

'Come,' he said, leading them out of the cave of statues and out of the stout door. 'I am going to bolt the men in. But I don't want to lock you in too.'

He shot all the bolts triumphantly. Crash! Crash! Crash! He'd done it! He'd done it!

28

The day after the storm

As soon as he had shot the bolts safely home, Jack col-
lapsed. His tussle with Pepi, his long run through the
wind and the rain, and the terrific excitement of making
the men prisoners had been too much for him. He sank
down on the steps outside the bolted door, and lay there
quite still.

It was dark there. The old couple felt about for Jack
in alarm. What was happening to the poor boy?

They found his torch in his pocket and took it out.
They switched it on and looked anxiously at Jack's pale
face and closed eyes. They tried to drag him up the steps.

'His clothes are wet,' said the old woman, feeling
Jack's soaked jersey and shorts. 'He will get a chill, a terrible chill. Maybe he will die of it. What shall we do, old
man?'

The old man answered her in her own language. 'We
will drag him up these steps. We will make him com-

fortable in the cave of stars. You shall wrap him in your shawl and he shall have my coat.'

Together the old couple managed to drag Jack up the steps. How they panted and groaned. They could not get him any further than the top. The old man stripped off Jack's wet things and put his coat round him. The old woman wrapped him all round in her thick shawl. They squeezed out his wet things and hung them on the rocky wall to dry.

They were frightened. What were they going to do now? Those men were bolted in the caves with what was left of their precious treasure. How angry they would be when they discovered what had happened!

Jack soon came to himself again. He sat up, wondering where he was. He had been in a kind of half faint, half asleep. He clutched at his clothes. What on earth had he got on? A shawl? Gracious, was he dressed up as a statue again?

The old people heard him moving and switched on the torch again. They looked anxiously at him and were relieved to see that he was no longer so white.

'You are better now?' asked the old man gently.

'Yes, thanks. I'm all right,' said Jack, pulling at the shawl. 'Whatever's this?'

'Your clothes were so wet,' said the old man. 'We had to take them off to dry them or you would have got a terrible chill. You have my coat and my wife's shawl.'

'Oh – well, thank you,' said Jack, feeling rather foolish in the coat and shawl. 'Sorry I gave you a fright. But I just conked out – that run up the mountainside, I suppose. I say – wasn't it a good idea bolting those men in?'

'Ah – but what will they do to us when they know?' said the old man sadly.

'Nothing! How can they?' said Jack. 'They are on the wrong side of the bolted door, aren't they? Don't you worry, we're all right!'

He got up. His legs were not very steady, but he could walk all right. 'I'm just going to the entrance of the caves to see if by any chance that awful wind storm has died down,' he said. 'If it has, I'll make my way to the fern cave, where the two girls are. They'll be scared by themselves.'

Somehow he stumbled along to the entrance. The clouds were so low and black that it was like night outside. Rain still swept over the hillside in great torrents. It was quite impossible to go out.

'I should get completely lost,' thought Jack. 'Golly, the girls will be so worried about me! I hope they won't be frightened all by themselves. Well, it's no use – I'll have to spend the night here with the old people – but it won't be very comfortable.'

It wasn't comfortable. They found a place in the cave of stars, a rounded, hollowed-out basin of rock, with only a few sharp edges. For the sake of warmth they all huddled together. Jack tried to make the old people take back their coat and shawl, saying that his clothes were almost dry.

But the old woman grew very angry when he suggested this, and scolded her husband hard in words that Jack could not understand, but whose meaning he could guess.

'My old one says that you are a bad bad boy to talk of putting on wet clothes,' said the old fellow. 'We will press close together. It is not cold in this cave.'

It wasn't very cold, it was true. Jack lay between the old man and his wife, looking up at the roof of the strange cave. He watched the curious greenish-blue stars shine and fade, flicker and glow. There were hundreds of them, most enchanting to watch. Jack wondered about them for a long time and then fell asleep.

In the morning the old people awoke first and felt stiff and uncomfortable. But they did not move for fear of disturbing Jack. He awoke at last and sat up. He saw the glowing stars above and around, and knew where he was at once.

'I wonder what the time is,' he said, looking at his watch. 'Half past seven! Gracious, I wonder what those men are doing! Are my clothes dry?'

Luckily they were. Jack put them on quickly, and gave back the coat and shawl with warm thanks. 'Now, you stay here a bit,' he said to the old couple. 'I'm just going to the bolted door to see if I can hear anything.'

He went off, feeling quite himself again now. As soon

as he came to the top of the curving stairway that led down to the oaken door, he heard bangs and crashes. Ah – the men had discovered that they were bolted in!

Crash! Bang! Thud! Smash!

They were hammering at the stout door for all they were worth. How they shouted and yelled, how they kicked at that door and tried to smash it down!

Jack stood at the top of the steps and grinned in delight. Serve them right! They were getting a taste of their own medicine. They had locked the children in – and now they themselves were prisoners.

Suddenly there was a loud bang that made Jack jump. It was a revolver shot. The men were shooting at the door, hoping to smash the bolts.

Bang! Bang! Bang!

Jack went back a little way, afraid that a bullet might glance off somehow and hit him, though this was impossible. BANG! BANG!

The bolts could not be smashed. The men gave the door a few more blows with something then stopped. Jack ran back to tell the old couple all about it.

But they were frightened, so it wasn't much fun telling them. 'I think I'll take you to the fern cave, where the girls are,' he told the old man. 'We have food and rugs in that cave. Come with me.'

The old couple wouldn't stir out of the place they knew so well. They were terrified of the open air, of the hillside and the outer world. They shrank back and nothing that Jack could say would make them change their minds.

'Well, I shall just have to go to the girls myself then,' said Jack at last. 'I'll bring them back here with food and rugs. We might as well all be together. Those men are no longer a danger to us. They can't possibly get out. Even if they find the hole behind that picture, I'm sure they won't get any further than the cave of echoes.'

He said good-bye to the frightened old people and went out into the sunshine. It was warm on his head and back – delicious. The sky was blue again, and the wind had gone.

He made his way to the waterfall, arriving there without any mistake, for he could follow the 'signposts' easily now. He was hailed by the girls as soon as they saw him. They were peeping out through the fern fronds.

'Jack! You didn't come back last night! Oh, Jack, I hardly slept at all, wondering what had happened to you,' cried Lucy-Ann.

'What happened?' asked Dinah, who was looking rather pale. She too had been very anxious, especially when the storm had come.

'Heaps!' said Jack. 'Marvellous news! Best in the world!'

'Gracious! Is Philip back then? – and Bill here?' cried Lucy-Ann at once.

'No – that's not my news,' said Jack. 'Do you know

what I've done? Bolted those men into the caves. What do you think of that?'

'What a *wonderful* idea!' said the girls together. 'But what about the old people?' asked Dinah.

'Oh, I got them out first,' said Jack. 'And I found Pepi back by the cowshed place, and tied him up properly. He's bound to that big tree where we once hid.'

'JACK! How marvellous you are!' cried Lucy-Ann. 'Did you fight him?'

'Well – not exactly,' said Jack. 'He caught me, and I kicked him hard. And just then the wind blew hard and a couple of our suitcases fell out of the tree and knocked him out. It was as much of a surprise to me as to him.'

'Oh – of course – we left our suitcases up there!' said Dinah. 'Oh, *Jack* – what a good thing we did!'

'Pepi must have had a most uncomfortable night,' said Jack. 'The rain and wind were his only companions.'

He told them how he had left the old couple in the cave of stars, and related the tale of the angry men trying to smash down the door.

'I can't get the old people to leave the caves,' he said. 'So we'd better take rugs and food and go back there to keep them company. They lent me their coat and shawl last night when my things were soaked. We can't leave them alone there without food or bedding.'

'Oh dear – I do like this cave so much better than anywhere else,' sighed Lucy-Ann. 'Still – those old people have been very good to us. Is Martha there too, Jack?'

'Golly! – no, I'd forgotten all about her,' said Jack, remembering. 'I hope those men don't kill and eat her.'

This was a dreadful thought, and made poor Lucy-Ann quite dumb for a minute or two. Poor Martha. Surely the men would leave her alone?

Kiki, of course, was as delighted to see Jack as the girls had been. She nestled on his shoulder, making crooning noises all the time he was talking, pulling at his ear and ruffling up his hair. Jack scratched her poll, delighted to have her again.

The girls collected a few tins, and Jack piled rugs over his shoulder. Then, with Kiki flying ahead, they set off to follow the familiar 'signposts' to the treasure caves. The sun beat down hotly. It was a really lovely day.

'I wish I could draw a plan of how that hole behind the picture leads to our fern cave,' said Dinah. 'The mountain is riddled with holes and caves. I say, isn't the waterfall loud this morning? – and it seems bigger than ever. I suppose it's all the rain last night.'

They arrived at the entrance to the caves at last and went in. They made their way to the cave of stars and the old couple greeted them warmly and joyfully. The old woman was full of delight to see Lucy-Ann again, and greeted her lovingly.

'I'm hungry,' said Lucy-Ann, trying to wriggle out of Elsa's arms. 'Very hungry.'

They all were. It was a strange place to have a meal in – the cave of stars. The children watched the flickering, shining lights, quite entranced by them. If only Lucy-Ann could take some home for her bedroom ceiling! She wished this once again as she watched the shining stars.

'Well, now, all we've got to do is to wait,' said Jack, arranging the pile of rugs for everyone to sit on as comfortably as possible. 'Everything rests with Philip now. Those men evidently don't know he hid in a plane or they would have said something. He must have escaped all right. What is he doing, I wonder?'

29

A very strange journey

What *had* happened to Philip? He was certainly having a most adventurous time.

He slept under the pile of coats and rugs in the plane until dawn. Then the planes landed, and bumped along the ground on their huge wheels. Philip awoke at once.

He made a peephole through the rugs and watched to see what the two men in his plane were doing. They were getting out. What a bit of luck that they hadn't even looked round the plane, or taken a coat from the pile!

Other men outside were greeting the new arrivals. Philip sat up and tried to hear what was said. But half of the speech was in a foreign language, and there was such a babel that it was impossible to make out anything.

He glanced round the plane. One of the crates was now in it, and a tarpaulin was tied loosely round it. Philip tried to see what was in it. Packed in straw was one of the statues, evidently one that was very valuable.

Philip peeped cautiously out of the window of the

plane, for now the men's voices had ceased. Where were the men? Could he slip out now and escape to get help?

He stared in surprise. The planes, and others too, were on a vast grassy plain – and in front and all round was the blue sea. All round! Well, then, they must be on some island somewhere.

He sat and thought for a moment. These men were rogues. They were doing a deal in valuable treasures hidden and perhaps forgotten during the last war; they had planes of their own – and a secret landing ground. What could be better than a lonely island, say, off the coast of Scotland?

'Then I suppose they'll have motor boats or launches of their own to get the stuff away,' thought Philip. 'A proper gang of them! I'll never get away from here without being seen – never. If it's an island – and it seems as if it must be – I'm as much a prisoner here as I was in the treasure caves. Blow!'

Then Dinah's idea came into his mind. What about hiding in the crate? That figure would be sure to be put on board a boat and shipped off somewhere to be sold. Well, couldn't he go with it?

He peeped out again to see where the men were. They were evidently having food and drink in a hut some distance off. Philip reckoned that he would have at least half an hour to get to work.

He loosened the tarpaulin a little more. He found that the crate was fastened by a hasp. He pulled it undone, and the whole side of the crate opened, like a sideways lid. Straw began to tumble out.

The figure was inside, packed loosely round with straw. Philip thought it must be the statue of some old-time saint. He looked at it closely. Could it be made of gold? It looked like it. Anyway, it didn't matter. It was going to lie where Philip had just been lying – under the pile of rugs and coats. And Philip was going to take its place.

It was not really very difficult to get the figure out of the straw, but it was heavy once it was out. Philip almost fell under its weight, though it was only about as big as he was himself.

He dragged it to the pile of rugs. He put it right underneath, and piled the things over it so that not a scrap of it showed. Then he cleared up the fallen bits of straw and pushed them carefully back into the crate.

Then he had the task of creeping into the straw himself. The statue had made quite a hole, and Philip settled down in the same place. He pulled the straw carefully round him, and dragged the sideways lid shut. But he could not fasten the hasp, and had to leave it, hoping that if the men saw it open they would simply think it had come undone by accident.

It was terribly warm in the straw. Philip began to be alarmed in case he might not be able to breathe after a time, and burrowed a little tunnel from his mouth and nose to the outside of the straw. After that he felt better.

He had been in the crate about a quarter of an hour when two men drove up in a cart. They unloaded all the planes. They carefully slid the crate that Philip was in out of the plane, and when the side swung open, fastened the hasp carefully. They did not guess for one moment that a live boy was inside, instead of a silent statue.

Philip's crate was loaded into the cart with other things. Then the cart was driven off towards the sea, bumping over ruts as it went. Philip was terribly jolted. The straw tickled and pricked him everywhere. He could hardly breathe.

But he didn't mind. He would soon be on board ship, and taken to the mainland somewhere. Then he could escape and go to the police. So he lay there patiently, trying to avoid the sharp prickles of the straw by wriggling about every now and again.

He could see nothing in the crate. He could only guess when the cart arrived at a small jetty, beside which a big launch was moored. He was carried on board and dumped on a lower deck.

Bump! Philip gasped, for he was very much shaken. Other things were dumped beside him. Then there came the sound of shouts and orders. The motor of the launch started up and Philip felt the vessel moving smoothly over the water. They were off!

'These men don't lose much time,' thought Philip.

'They don't have these things on their hands very long. Wonder who buys them?'

The trip to the mainland, wherever it was, was a long one. Philip was now quite sure that the landing ground for the planes was on some lonely island. At last the launch eased into some kind of harbour and came to a stop. Men began to unload it at once.

The crate was rather roughly handled, and once poor Philip was put upside-down for half a minute. That was terrible. He thought he would have to call out. But just when he was certain he couldn't bear it any longer, he felt the crate being lifted again and put on a car or into a van, which drove off almost immediately.

After a while it stopped. Philip heard the sound of an engine whistling and his heart leapt for joy. They were probably at a railway station. Perhaps he would be put into the luggage van – or on a goods train. It would be easy enough to escape then. He had not dared to before, for he had felt certain that all the men handling the crate so far had been accomplices of the others.

He was not put on a train. He was left in a yard, along with other goods that were to go by a later train. He strained his ears, hoping to hear the van being driven off. Then, he thought, it would be safe for him to get out.

He waited for about twenty minutes. Then he began to try and wriggle out. But he could not undo the hasp. Blow!

He yelled. 'Hi! Hi! Help me!'

A porter not far off jumped in alarm. He looked all round. There was no one in sight except a solitary passenger waiting for the next train, and another porter on the opposite platform.

Philip yelled again, 'Hi! Hi! Let me out!'

The porter felt terribly scared. He looked at the waiting passenger. Had he heard the shouts too – or was it just the porter's own imagination? The passenger *had* heard them, and he was looking most alarmed.

'Somebody in trouble somewhere,' said the man, walking to the porter. 'Sounds as if he's in that little yard there.'

'There's nobody there,' said the porter, staring into the yard.

'Hi! Hurry up and let me out!' came Philip's urgent voice, and to the horror of the passenger and the porter, the big crate began to rock violently.

'There's someone in there!' cried the porter, and ran to the crate. He undid the hasp with trembling fingers and out came Philip, straw in his hair, straw down his neck, straw all over him, looking wild and terribly excited.

'I want the police station,' said Philip. 'Can't stop to explain anything to you now. Where's the police station?'

'Over there,' stuttered the porter, pointing to a small square building about a hundred yards away from the railway station. 'But – but – but . . .'

Philip left him 'but-ing' away, and sped off to the

police station, thrilled at his escape. He had managed it wonderfully, he thought.

He shot into the police station and almost scared the policeman there out of his life.

'I want to report something important to somebody in authority,' said Philip. 'Who's the head man here?'

'I'm the constable here,' said the policeman. 'Who are you, and what do you want? You can report to me.'

'I want to use the telephone,' said Philip, thinking it would be a good thing to get into touch with Bill at once. 'Will you get a number for me, please?'

'Here here – you can't go using our police phones without good cause,' said the policeman, beginning to feel that this straw-strewn boy was mad. 'What's your name, and where do you live?'

'My name is Philip Mannering,' said Philip impatiently. 'Don't hold me up, please. I've very important things to report to somebody.'

The name caught the policeman's attention at once. 'Philip Mannering?' he said. 'Here – are you one of the missing children? There's four been missing for days. You one of them?'

He drew a leaflet from a drawer and looked at it. He passed it across to Philip. To the boy's surprise he saw a photograph of himself, Lucy-Ann, Jack and Dinah – and Kiki too, of course – at the head of the paper, and their names and descriptions underneath.

'Yes – I'm that boy,' he said, pointing to his photograph. 'Philip Mannering. And I want to get in touch with Bill Smugs – no, his real name's Cunningham, of course – at once. It's MOST IMPORTANT.'

The policeman suddenly got very busy. He took up the receiver of the phone. He barked a number into it, which he got at once. He evidently got on to somebody in high authority immediately.

'Sir, one of the missing children has just turned up here – Philip Mannering – wants to report something to Detective Inspector Cunningham. Yes, sir. I will, sir.' He turned to Philip.

'Are the other children with you?'

'No – but they're all right – so far,' said Philip. 'I've escaped and I want help to rescue them. Can I get on to Bill Cunningham, please?'

The policeman spoke into the telephone. 'The other children are all right, but not with him. Please notify Mrs Mannering. More news to follow. When will the Inspector be here?'

The policeman put the receiver down and gazed in a very pleased manner at Philip. To think that this exciting case of Missing Children should be reported to *his* little station!

'Where am I?' asked Philip suddenly. 'What is this place called?'

'Don't you know?' said the policeman, surprised. 'It's Gairdon, on the north-east coast of Scotland.'

'I guessed that's about where I'd be,' said Philip.

'Sorry I can't tell you anything, constable – but I think I'd better wait for Bill.'

Bill came – in his aeroplane! He landed at the nearest aerodrome, took a fast police car, and arrived at Gairdon in two hours' time. Very good going. Philip heard the car roaring up and ran to meet it.

'Bill! I knew you'd come! Oh, Bill – I've got the most exciting news for you! I don't know where to begin.'

30

Bill gets busy

Bill swung out of the car, took hold of Philip by the arm and had a good look at him. 'You're all right?' he demanded. 'All of you? Your mother's been nearly off her head with worry.'

'I'm all right, Bill, so's everybody. But we've fallen right into the middle of a most extraordinary adventure,' said Philip. 'I must tell you quickly. We've got to get busy. You see . . .'

'Come into the police station,' said Bill. Philip followed the burly figure, full of relief to hear his determined voice, and to see his strong, clever face.

Soon the whole story was being poured out. Bill listened in amazement, occasionally rapping out a sharp question. When he heard how Philip had taken the statue out of the crate and put himself in its place, and was taken to the railway station, he burst out laughing.

'I never in my life knew children like you! Whatever will you do next? I can't cope with you. But, joking apart, this is a most extraordinary thing, Philip, most amazing. The men you got caught up with are the very men I'd been after for some time. We couldn't find out what they were up to – though we knew jolly well they were up to no good.'

'Really?' said Philip, astonished. 'By the way, Bill – that night we were to go with you in your plane – and got into the wrong one – we heard shots. Was that anything to do with you?'

'It was,' said Bill grimly. 'It so happened that two of the men were spotted there, and detained. They shot their way out – and that was what you heard. I nearly got a bullet in my leg. I can tell you, we shall be very glad to get our hands on them and have something to charge them with. Clever rogues! They are crooks from South America, in touch with the old Nazis, who have told them the whereabouts of many of the lost or hidden treasures in Europe. Many of them have never been found, you know.'

'Gosh – you wait till you see our treasure caves!' said Philip. 'Oh – by the way, here's a notebook I pinched from one of the men's coats.'

He handed it over. Bill squinted at it, and his eyes nearly fell out of his head.

'I say – my word! – look here – this is a code – the code the rascals use – and a list of all the people concerned in this racket – with their addresses in code!

Philip, you deserve a medal. This is a first-class find. We can round up the whole gang.'

Philip was delighted at Bill's pleasure. Bill got up and went to the telephone. He made many calls, short, sharp and to the point. Philip listened but could not make much of them. He hoped Bill would soon set off to rescue the others. They would be waiting most anxiously.

Bill put down the telephone receiver at last. 'We're taking my aeroplane and another, and twelve men counting myself,' he said. 'Starting at twelve.'

'I'm going too, aren't I?' said Philip anxiously.

'I think you'd better stay and see your mother,' said Bill. 'And also – there may be a bit of a dust-up, you know, when we get there.'

Philip stared at him in the greatest indignation. 'Bill! The others will be there – Jack and the rest – and you'd keep *me* out of it? Didn't I come here, didn't I . . .'

'All right, all right, old son,' said Bill. 'You shall come. Goodness knows what further adventure you'd get into if I left you behind.'

Philip cheered up at once. He took Lizzie out of his pocket and introduced her to Bill. 'Meet busy Dizzy Lizzie,' he said, and Lizzie ran on to Bill's knee.

'Sounds like Kiki's make-up,' said Bill. 'Busy Dizzy Lizzie! What a name for a lizard!'

'I suppose we can't get anything to eat here, can we?' asked Philip, wondering if there were ever any eatables at a police station. 'I've had chocolate to nibble at times, but that's all.'

'I was going to suggest that we should ask the good constable here to provide us with a really slap-up meal,' said Bill. 'We could go to the hotel, but you don't look very presentable at the moment – you seem to exude bits of straw from top to toe. We'll have a good meal and then give you a wash and brush-up.'

The wind got up as they ate their meal. Bill stared out of the window. 'Hope this wind dies down,' he said. 'Looks a bit stormy to me.'

Bill was right. Just before it was time for them to set off in the car to the aerodrome, the telephone rang. Bill answered it. He listened gravely and turned to Philip.

'There's a gale warning out,' he said. 'Afraid it's no good starting off yet, Philip. Very stormy weather where we want to go.'

'Blow!' said Philip, disappointed and anxious. 'The others will be so worried, waiting and waiting for us.'

'Yes, they will,' said Bill. 'But the aerodrome doesn't give out warnings like this without reason. They are apparently expecting one of those sudden gale-storms that mean a plane must fly absolutely blind. Not so funny. We'll have to wait a bit.'

Philip looked upset. It would be too awful if those men got back to the valley before they did and perhaps caught the others. And he did so badly want Bill to catch the men red-handed – wanted him to get there before them and wait for them to come again and take away the treasures.

'By the way, Bill – how do you know where to fly to?' he asked suddenly. '*I* didn't know what the valley was – or where – except that it is in Austria. Elsa and the old man told us that.'

'It's down in that interesting little notebook you gave me,' said Bill, 'together with other places where they may also find hidden treasures. Oh, that notebook told me quite a lot I wanted to know, Philip.'

Bill got out a map and showed Philip exactly where the valley was. 'It had a bad time in the war,' he said, 'and the only pass into it was bombed. It hasn't been unblocked again, as far as I know. Plans were afoot to work on it this year. A man called Julius Muller – the one you were told to get in touch with – has been trying to get permission to unblock the valley and enter it.'

'I wonder what happened to Otto,' said Philip. 'The poor prisoner, you know.'

'His address is in the book,' said Bill. 'I have already asked for information about him, I daresay I shall get some soon.'

He did. The telephone rang that afternoon and a voice informed Bill that Otto Engler had been found outside a big hospital, unconscious. He had almost died of heart trouble, but was making slight progress now, though he could not speak a word.

'I bet those brutes ill-treated him and made him tell

them the exact whereabouts of the treasure caves,' said Philp, 'and then took him and left him somewhere in the street, ill and terrified.'

'Quite likely,' agreed Bill. 'They wouldn't stop at much.' The telephone bell rang again, and Bill took up the receiver once more.

'Gale getting worse,' he told Philip. 'Have to put off our trip till tomorrow. Pity your mother's so far away or we could have dropped in to see her. I've been trying to get her on the phone.'

Philip did speak to his mother that afternoon, though it was only a three minute talk. Mrs Mannering was so relieved to hear his voice that she could hardly say a word herself. However, Philip found plenty to say, and had to stop halfway through because he was cut off.

Next day dawned fair and warm. The wind had almost gone – blown itself out in the night, which had been extremely stormy and wild. Philip had awakened once or twice and had felt glad they had not tried to fly through it, for certainly it was a very wild storm.

He had slept in a comfortable bed put up in the cell of the police station. This seemed very exciting to him. 'First time I've ever passed a night in prison,' he told Bill.

'Well, I hope it will be the last,' said Bill. 'Prison is not a pleasant place, my boy.'

Bill's car was brought to the door. It was large and bright and swift. He and Philip got in, Bill started up the engine and they roared away. Twenty, thirty, forty, fifty, sixty, seventy miles an hour and more! Philip was thrilled.

'She does go,' he said. 'Funny that a car seems faster than an aeroplane when you're in it. Much more of a rush, somehow.'

They reached the aerodrome at last. There was Bill's plane, its propellers whirring fast. Beside it was another, very like it. Eleven men stood about, waiting. They saluted Bill.

'Get into my plane,' Bill ordered Philip. 'I want a word with my men.'

He had his word and got in. Five of the men got in Bill's plane and six in the other. There was a terrific roar, and first Bill's plane took off and then the other one. They flew into the wind, circled round, rose higher and then made off for the east.

Philip gave a sigh of relief. Now things were on the move again. He would soon see the others. How glad they would be!

After some time Bill spoke to Philip. 'We're coming to that valley of yours, Philip, now – or should be. Have a look out and see if you recognise it.'

Philip looked down. 'Oh yes!' he cried. 'That's it! And look – there are four planes down there! That's where we land! You'd better look out in case the men are about and shoot!'

Bill's plane roared down lower. It swung into the

wind and landed perfectly. The second plane followed suit.

The engines stopped. There was silence. Bill waited to see if anyone came running out. No, not a soul. He and the other men poured out. Philip followed.

There seemed to be no one about at all. Bill told his men to scatter and make a search before they went any further. Soon one of them gave a shout. 'Hey! There's one of them here! All tied up like a chicken!'

It was Pepi, half dead with cold and hunger. He was so glad to be set free that he did not show much surprise at seeing so many strangers. In charge of one of the men he tottered over to Bill.

'Put him in the hut and lock him up,' ordered Bill. 'Who could have tied him up, Philip?'

'I can't imagine,' said Philip, puzzled. 'And look, Bill, here are two of our suitcases – fallen out of the tree, I suppose. Funny.'

'There are still seven men to be accounted for,' said Bill. 'Right. Well, now – we'd better set off to these treasure caves. Look out, men, in case there's any ambush. We don't want to be shot up without warning.'

They set off, Philip telling Bill the way. Bill was filled with amazement to see the valley, the towering mountains, the burnt ruins . . . it seemed so extraordinary to think of the four children marooned here in the middle of such thrilling adventures.

'Can you hear the waterfall now?' asked Philip eagerly, after a time. 'I can! We're getting near.'

The men were amazed to hear the noise of the great waterfall, and even more astonished to see it. They did not say very much, for they were tough men, not easily surprised by anything. But they stood and stared for some time.

'Now – careful – because we're getting near to the cave entrance,' said Philip at last. 'Shall I go first? I think I'd better.'

31

An exciting finish

Jack, Dinah, Lucy-Ann, Kiki and the old couple were still in the cave of stars. They had just finished their meal, and were wondering what to do. What a pity the old couple wouldn't come outside the mountain – it was such a lovely day!

'We could easily go and sun ourselves there,' said Lucy-Ann longingly. 'There's no danger from those men. They can't get out of that locked door.'

Just as she spoke, Jack clutched hold of her arm and made her jump. 'Sh! I can hear voices.'

They all listened fearfully. Yes – there *were* voices – coming down the tunnel that led from the cave of stalactites to the cave they were now in.

'More men! Quick, hide!' said Dinah urgently. In a panic the children began to run to the other end of the cave, stumbling and tripping, their feet echoing round the big vault.

'Halt!' cried a stern voice, and a big figure stood just inside the cave. 'Stand still! Put your hands up!'

Lucy-Ann knew that voice. Of course she did. 'Bill! BILL!' she squealed. 'Oh, Bill, we thought you were never coming!'

She ran across the cave and flung herself on the surprised Bill. Jack and Dinah followed, shouting in delight. Lucy-Ann caught sight of Philip and flung herself on him too.

'Philip! Dear Philip, you did escape and get Bill!'

Philip was astonished to see the children and the old couple there. He had left them in the treasure caves. How had they got out? And where were the men?

The old couple came slowly up, half frightened to see so many people by the light of the powerful torches. Bill was gentle with them.

'Poor frightened moles,' he said to Philip. 'Well, they will be well looked after and rewarded. Now – where are these men?'

'I bolted them in,' said Jack proudly. 'They are prisoners in the treasure caves.'

This was news to Philip – and, of course, to Bill too. They questioned Jack eagerly, and he told them how the old woman had shown them the hole behind the picture, and how they had managed to escape through it to the cave of echoes and from there to their own fern cave. Then how Jack had gone to the men's hut, and had come up against Pepi and tied him up – finally how he had got his Great Idea, and slipped back to bolt the men in.

'Well – that seems pretty good work to me!' said Bill. 'But it won't be an easy job routing them out of those caves. I wonder if we could take them by surprise from the back – get in at the picture-hole and give them a shock.'

'Oh *yes*!' said Jack. 'Of course you could. You could leave one or two of your men at the bolted door here, attracting the attention of the seven men – and whilst they are shouting and yelling at one another, the rest of your men could go in the other way and surprise them.'

'That seems a very sound plan,' said Bill, and gave some orders. He turned to Philip. 'I'm leaving two men here. Take them to the bolted door in half an hour's time, and they will then attract the men's attention. Jack, you come with me and the others, and show me the way back to your fern cave, and through the cave of echoes to the passage that leads to the hole at the back of that picture.'

The little procession set off. The two men left behind waited for half an hour and then went with Philip to the bolted door at the bottom of the curving steps. They rapped on it and shouted.

An answering shout came from inside. 'Who are you? Let us out! Open the door!'

The men inside banged at the door and the men outside did the same. It was a perfect babel of noise. All the seven men were there, arguing, banging, demanding to be set free, and generally losing their tempers.

Meantime Bill, Jack and the others had gone to the fern cave. They had crawled in, and found to their dismay that they had to wriggle through the drain-pipe hole at the back. One of them almost got stuck.

'I must say you children manage to get into the most marvellous scrapes,' said Bill, emerging from the hole into the cave of echoes. 'My, I'm hot!'

'Hot, hot, HOT, HOT!' said the echoes at once. Bill jumped. 'What's that?'

'That, that, THAT, THAT!' shouted the echoes alarmingly. Jack laughed. 'It's only the echoes,' he said. Kiki began to squawk, and then whistled like an express engine. The noise was deafening.

'Kiki always does that here,' said Jack, leading the way. 'Shut up, Kiki! Bad bird!'

Soon they were in the passage that led to behind the waterfall – but before they got there they came to the hole in the roof.

'Have you got a rope on you, Bill?' said Jack. 'We've got to get up here. I used my rope to tie up Pepi. If you can get me on your shoulder, and shove me up, I can crawl into the hole, fix the rope and let it down.'

It was soon done. One after another the men crawled into the hole, thinking that never in their lives had they done so much climbing, creeping and crawling. They looked at Jack in admiration. What a boy!

Jack came to the hole behind the picture. He listened. Not a sound. The men were all at the bolted door, shouting, kicking and arguing.

Jack gave the picture a push and it fell. The room was empty. He jumped down and the others followed one by one.

'Hope there's no more of this, sir,' said one of the men to Bill. 'You want thinner men for this job.'

'Better go cautiously now,' said Jack. 'We are near the treasure caves. We go straight through three and then come to the cave of statues. That's where the bolted door is.'

'Quiet now,' ordered Bill, and, treading softly in their rubber-soled shoes, the men moved slowly forward, revolvers glinting in their hands.

Through the cave of gold – through the cave of books – through the cave of pictures. Jack laid his hand warningly on Bill's arm. He could hear something.

'It's the men,' he said. 'Hark! – they must have got rocks or something to hammer at the door like that. They really will break it down, I should think, by the noise.'

Bill stepped from the tunnel into the cave of statues. Although he had been prepared for them by Philip, he could not help jumping a little when he saw them in that dim greenish glow. His men stepped silently behind him.

At the far end were the seven men. They had found a

big rock and were using it as a battering-ram. Crash! It struck the door violently. Crash!

'Now's our chance,' whispered Bill. 'They have their hands full – not a revolver to be seen among them. Come on!'

The men moved swiftly up behind Juan and the others. A sharp, stern voice barked out behind them:

'Hands up! We've got you cold!'

The men all had their backs to Bill. At his voice, they jumped in surprise, and put their hands above their heads at once. Then Juan swung round, his hands still high. His eyes swept the stern group of men in front of him.

'How did you get here?' he said, between his teeth. 'What other way in is there? Who locked us in?'

'No questions answered now,' snapped Bill. He called loudly to the two men outside the door.

'Hey, Jim! Pete! Unbolt the door. We've got 'em.'

The door was unbolted. It swung open and Jim and Pete looked round it, grinning. 'Pretty little play we had,' said Pete. 'Quite enjoyed it, I did.'

Jack slipped down too. The girls had been told to keep away till the men had been captured. They were with the old couple in the cave of stars, waiting impatiently.

Bill counted the men. 'All seven here. Good. And we've got the eighth all right too. Pete, take these fellows back to the planes. Shoot at the first sign of trouble. I'll stay here and have a look-see. It looks mighty interesting.'

The men were marched off, handcuffed, swearing and stumbling. Jack watched them go, delighted to think that he had had the idea of bolting them in. Bill had clapped him on the back for that.

Once the men had passed through the cave of stars, the girls came running to join Jack, Philip and Bill. They showed the astonished Bill everything. He whistled when he saw so many treasures.

'Fortunes here,' he said. 'Well, it won't be an easy task finding out where all these things came from and sending them back. Perhaps Julius Muller can help.'

'And the old couple can too,' said Lucy-Ann eagerly. 'They know the histories of most of the statues, anyway.'

The old man and his wife were collected on the way out and taken with everyone else to the planes. They made no objection now to going into the open air. They evidently thought that Bill was some Great Man Who Must Be Obeyed. They bowed to him whenever he spoke to them.

'We'll have to take them with us for questioning,' said Bill. 'But we'll return them as soon as possible – to the village where this good man, Julius, lives. He may be good enough to look after these old people.'

Everyone got into one or other of the planes. There were six of them. In three of them were the eight prisoners with their guards. In two others were pilots and the old couple. Bill's plane carried the children.

Their plane rose up, and the children looked down at the strange valley for the last time.

'Yes, have a good look,' said Bill. It will be in all the papers presently – the Valley of Treasure.'

'No, Bill – the Valley of Adventure!' said Jack. 'That's what *we* shall always call it – the Valley of Adventure!'

'I'm glad we found Martha all right,' said Lucy-Ann suddenly. 'I did like her so much. She was sweet.'

'Good heavens! Who's Martha?' said Bill, startled. 'I thought the old woman was called Elsa. Don't tell me Martha is someone we've left behind!'

'Oh no, Bill – she's sitting on Elsa's knee now in one of the other planes – she might even lay an egg there,' said Lucy-Ann.

Bill looked even more astonished. 'She's a *hen*!' explained Lucy-Ann. 'She got left behind in the caves with the men and we were afraid she might have been killed by them. But she wasn't. She hid under the table and came clucking to join us when we went to find her. You were busy looking at the gold, I expect.'

'I must have missed her,' said Bill. 'To think I haven't yet made the acquaintance of one of the ladies in this thrilling adventure. What a pity!'

'What a pity, what a pity, what a pity!' said Kiki at once. 'Cluck-luck-luck! Pop goes Martha!'

Don't miss . . .

The *Sea*
of adventure

*the next exciting book in Enid Blyton's
thrilling Adventure series*

1

No governess, thank you!

'Do you know, it's May the fifth already!' said Jack, in a very gloomy voice. 'All the fellows will be back at school today.'

'What a pity, what a pity!' said Kiki the parrot, in just as gloomy a voice as Jack's.

'This awful measles!' said Lucy-Ann. 'First Philip had it as soon as he came home for the hols, then Dinah, then she gave it to me, and then you had it!'

'Well, we're all out of quarantine now,' said Dinah, from her corner of the room. 'It's just silly of the doctor to say we ought to go away and have a change before we go back to school. Isn't it enough change to go back to school? I do so love the summer term too.'

'Yes – and I bet I'd have been in the first eleven,' said Philip, pushing back the tuft of hair he had in front. 'Golly, I'll be glad to get my hair cut again! It feels tickly, now it's grown so long!'

The four children had all had a bad attack of measles

in the holidays. Jack especially had had a very nasty time, and Dinah's eyes had given her a lot of trouble. This was partly her own fault, for she had been forbidden to read, and had disobeyed the doctor's orders. Now her eyes kept watering, and she blinked in any bright light.

'Certainly no school work for Dinah yet,' the doctor had said sternly. 'I suppose you thought you knew better than I did, young lady, when you disobeyed orders. Think yourself lucky if you don't have to wear glasses a little later on!'

'I hope Mother won't send us away to some awful boarding-house by the sea,' said Dinah. 'She can't come with us herself, because she's taken on some kind of important job for the summer. I hope she doesn't get us a governess or something to take us away.'

'A *governess*!' said Philip in scorn. 'I jolly well wouldn't go. And anyway she wouldn't stay now that I'm training young rats.'

His sister Dinah looked at him in disgust. Philip always had some kind of creature about him, for he had a great love of animals. He could do anything he liked with them, and Lucy-Ann secretly thought that if he met a roaring tiger in a jungle, he would simply hold out his hand, and the tiger would lick it like a dog, and purr happily like a cat.

'I've told you, Philip, that if you so much as let me see one of your young rats I'll scream!' Dinah said.

'All right, then scream!' said Philip obligingly. 'Hey, Squeaker, where are you?'

Squeaker appeared above the neck of Philip's jersey collar, and true to his name squeaked loudly. Dinah screamed.

'You beast, Philip! How many of those things have you got down your neck? If we had a cat I'd give them all to her.'

'Well, we haven't,' said Philip, and poked Squeaker's head down his collar again.

'Three blind mice,' remarked Kiki the parrot, with great interest, cocking her head on one side and watching for Squeaker to appear again.

'Wrong, Kiki, old bird,' said Jack, lazily putting out a hand and pulling at his parrot's tail feathers. 'Far from being three blind mice, it's one very wide-awake rat. I say, Kiki, why didn't you catch measles from us?'

Kiki was quite prepared to have a conversation with Jack. She gave a loud cackle, and then put her head down to be scratched. 'How many times have I told you to shut the door?' she cried. 'How many times have I told you to wipe your feet? Wipe the door, shut your feet, wipe the . . .'

'Hey, you're getting muddled!' said Jack and the others laughed. It was always comical when Kiki mixed up the things she loved to say. The parrot liked to make people laugh. She raised her head, put up her crest, and made a noise like a mowing-machine outside in the garden.

'That's enough,' said Jack, tapping her on the beak. 'Now stop it, Kiki!'

But Kiki, pleased with the noise, flew up to the top of the curtains, and went on being a mowing-machine, one that wanted oiling.

Mrs Mannering put her head in at the door. 'Children! Don't let Kiki make such a noise. I'm interviewing someone, and it's very annoying.'

'Who's come for an interview?' said Philip at once. 'Mother! You haven't gone and got a governess or something awful to take us away for a change, have you? Is she here?'

'Yes, she is,' said Mrs Mannering. All the children groaned. 'Well, dears, you know I can't spare the time to take you myself,' she went on. 'I've taken on this new job, though, of course, if I'd known you were going to be measly for so long, and then be so peaky afterwards . . .'

'We're *not* peaky!' said Philip indignantly. 'What an awful word!'

'Peaky Squeaky,' said Kiki at once, and cackled with laughter. She loved putting the same-sounding words together. 'Peaky Squeaky!'

'Shut up, Kiki!' called Jack, and threw a cushion at her. 'Aunt Allie – we can quite well go away by ourselves. We're old enough to look after ourselves perfectly.'

'Jack, as soon as I let you out of my sight in the

holidays, you plunge into the middle of the most hair-raising adventures,' said Mrs Mannering. 'I shan't forget what happened in the last summer holidays – going off in the wrong aeroplane and being lost for ages in a strange valley.'

'Oh, that was a *marvellous* adventure!' cried Philip. 'I wish we could have another. I'm fed up with being measly so long. Do, do let us go away by ourselves, Mother, there's a darling!'

'No,' said his mother. 'You're going to a perfectly safe seaside spot with a perfectly safe governess for a perfectly safe holiday.'

'Safe, safe, safe!' shrieked Kiki. 'Sound and safe, sound and safe!'

'Other way round, Kiki,' said Jack. Mrs Mannering put her fingers to her ears.

'That bird! I suppose I'm tired with nursing you all, but honestly Kiki gets dreadfully on my nerves just now. I shall be glad when she's gone with you.'

'I bet no governess will like Kiki,' said Jack. 'Aunt Allie, have you told her about Kiki?'

'Not yet,' admitted Mrs Mannering. 'But I suppose I'd better bring her in and introduce her to you all and to Kiki too.'

She went out. The children scowled at one another. 'I knew it would happen. Instead of having fun at school we shall mope about with somebody we can't bear,' said Dinah gloomily. 'Phil – can't you do something with those awful rats of yours when she comes in? If she knew you were the kind of boy that likes mice and rats and beetles and hedgehogs living down his neck and in his pockets, she'd probably run for miles.'

'Jolly good idea, Dinah!' said everyone at once, and Philip beamed at her. 'It's not often you get a brainwave,' he said, 'but that's one all right. Hey, Squeaker! Come along out. Woffles, where are you? Nosey, come out of my pocket!'

Dinah retreated to the furthest corner of the room, watching the young white rats in horror. However many had Philip got? She determined not to go near him if she could possibly help it.

'I think Kiki might perform also,' said Jack, grinning. 'Kiki – puff-puff-puff!'

That was the signal for the parrot to do her famous imitation of a railway engine screeching in a tunnel. She opened her beak and swelled out her throat in delight. It wasn't often that she was begged to make this fearful noise. Lucy-Ann put her hands to her ears.

The door opened and Mrs Mannering came in with a tall, rather stern-looking woman. It was quite plain that no adventure, nothing unusual, would ever be allowed to happen anywhere near Miss Lawson. 'Perfectly safe' was written all over her.

'Children, this is Miss Lawson,' began Mrs Mannering, and then her voice was drowned in Kiki's railway-engine screech. It was an even better imitation than usual, and longer drawn-out. Kiki was really letting herself go.

Miss Lawson gave a gasp and took a step backwards. At first she did not see Kiki, but looked at the children, thinking that one of them must be making the terrible noise.

'KIKI!' thundered Mrs Mannering, really angry. 'Children, how could you let her? I'm ashamed of you!'

Kiki stopped. She put her head on one side and looked cheekily at Miss Lawson. 'Wipe your feet!' she commanded. 'Shut the door! Where's your handkerchief? How many times have I told you to . . .'

'Take Kiki out, Jack,' said Mrs Mannering, red with annoyance. 'I'm so sorry, Miss Lawson. Kiki belongs to Jack, and she isn't usually so badly behaved.'

'I see,' said Miss Lawson, looking very doubtful. 'I'm not very much used to parrots, Mrs Mannering. I suppose, of course, that this bird will not come away with us? I could not be responsible for pets of that kind – and I don't think that a boarding-house . . .'

'Well, we can discuss that later,' said Mrs Mannering hastily. 'Jack, did you hear what I said? Take Kiki out.'

'Polly, put the kettle on,' said Kiki to Miss Lawson, who took absolutely no notice at all. Kiki growled like a very fierce dog, and Miss Lawson looked startled. Jack caught the parrot, winked at the others and took Kiki out of the room.

'What a pity, what a pity!' mourned Kiki as the door shut behind them. Mrs Mannering gave a sigh of relief.

'Jack and Lucy-Ann Trent are not my own children,' she said to Miss Lawson. 'Lucy-Ann, shake hands with Miss Lawson. Lucy-Ann and her brother are great friends of my own children, and they live with us, and all go off to boarding-school together,' she explained.

Miss Lawson looked at the green-eyed, red-haired little girl and liked her. She was very like her brother, she thought. Then she looked at Philip and Dinah, each dark-eyed and dark-haired, with a queer tuft that stuck up in front. She would make them brush it down properly, thought Miss Lawson.

Dinah came forward politely and shook hands. She thought that Miss Lawson would be very proper, very strict and very dull – but oh, so safe!

Then Philip came forward, but before he could shake hands, he clutched at his neck. Then he clutched at one leg of his shorts. Then he clapped a hand over his middle. Miss Lawson stared at him in amazement.

'Excuse me – it's only my rats,' explained Philip, and to Miss Lawson's enormous horror she saw Squeaker running round his collar, Nosey making a lump here and there over his tummy, and Woffles coming out of his sleeve. Goodness, how many more had the awful boy got!

'I'm sorry,' said Miss Lawson faintly. 'I'm very sorry – but I can't take this post, Mrs Mannering. I really can't.'

*Read all the exciting adventures
in this bestselling series*

The  of adventure

Something very sinister is happening on the mysterious Isle of Gloom and the children are determined to uncover the truth!

But Philip, Dinah, Lucy-Ann and Jack are not prepared for the dangerous adventure that awaits them in the abandoned copper mines and secret tunnels beneath the sea.

The  of adventure

Why is everyone so afraid of the castle on the hill, and what dark secrets lurk inside its walls?

When flashing lights are seen in a distant tower, Philip, Dinah, Lucy-Ann and Jack decide to investigate – and discover a very sinister plot concealed within its hidden rooms and gloomy underground passages.

The
of adventure

Who are the two strange pilots, and what is the secret treasure hidden in the lonely valley where the children land?

Nothing could be more exciting than a daring night flight on Bill's plane! But Philip, Dinah, Lucy-Ann and Jack soon find themselves flying straight into a truly amazing adventure.

The
of adventure

A mysterious trip to the desolate Northern Isles soon turns into a terrifying adventure when Bill is kidnapped!

Marooned far from the mainland on a deserted coast, Philip, Dinah, Lucy-Ann and Jack find themselves playing a dangerous game with an unknown enemy. Will they escape with Bill and their lives?

The *Mountain* of adventure

Surely a peaceful holiday in the Welsh mountains will keep the children out of trouble! But the mystery of a rumbling mountain soon has them thirsty for more adventure.

Philip, Dinah, Lucy-Ann and Jack are determined to explore the mountain and uncover its secret, but first they must escape from a pack of ravenous wolves and a mad genius who plans to rule the world!

The *Ship* of adventure

An amazing voyage around the beautiful Greek islands becomes an exciting quest to find the lost treasure of the Andra!

Philip, Dinah, Lucy-Ann and Jack are plunged into a search for hidden riches – with some ruthless villains hot on their trail! Will they find the treasure before it's too late?

The *Circus* of adventure

Why did Bill have to bring the babyish Gustavus with them on holiday? Jack knows he'll only be trouble . . .

But when Gustavus is kidnapped, along with Philip, Dinah and Lucy-Ann, Jack bravely sets out to rescue them, leading him to a faraway land and the discovery of a plot to kill the King!

The *River* of adventure

A river cruise through ancient desert lands becomes a mysterious adventure when Bill disappears!

While Philip, Dinah, Lucy-Ann and Jack are desperately searching for Bill, they become trapped beneath a forgotten temple where no one has set foot for 7,000 years. What dangers lurk within, and will they ever escape?

A selected list of titles available from Macmillan Children's Books

The prices shown below are correct at the time of going to press. However, Macmillan Publishers reserves the right to show new retail prices on covers, which may differ from those previously advertised.

All Pan Macmillan titles can be ordered from our website, www.panmacmillan.com, or from your local bookshop and are also available by post from:

Bookpost, PO Box 29, Douglas, Isle of Man IM99 1BQ

Credit cards accepted. For details:
Telephone: 01624 677237
Fax: 01624 670923
Email: bookshop@enterprise.net
www.bookpost.co.uk

Free postage and packing in the United Kingdom